MONKEY MADNESS

Anna Wilson lives in Bradford on Avon with her husband, two children, two cats, one dog and six chickens. She is the author of many young-fiction novels published by Macmillan Children's Books – and while many of them have been about pets, this is the first to feature wild African monkeys.

MONKEY MADNESS

THE ONLY WAY IS AFRICA!

Anna Wilson

ILLUSTRATED BY ANDY ROWLAND

MACMILLAN CHILDREN'S BOOKS

First published 2014 by Macmillan Children's Books
a division of Macmillan Publishers Limited
20 New Wharf Road, London N1 9RR
Basingstoke and Oxford
Associated companies throughout the world
www.panmacmillan.com

ISBN 978-1-4472-3664-1

1 3 5 7 9 8 6 4 2

A CIP catalogue record for this book is available from
the British Library.

Printed and bound by CPI Group (UK) Ltd, Croydon CR0 4YY

For the real Bibi, who took us on an amazing
safari in Botswana and told us wonderful
stories about animals and his life.

Ke a leboga, Rra!

CHAPTER 1

A BIT OF A MISUNDERSTANDING

As soon as Flo discovered about the trip to Africa she said, 'We absolutely have to start practising with the camera.'

Felix chewed his bottom lip. 'When you say "we" . . .' he began.

But Flo was not listening. 'Everyone knows that it is important to practise with Technological Equipment before you try it In The Field.'

Felix frowned. 'But I'm not going into a field. I'm going to Botswana, which is in east Africa. I don't think they have fields. They have The Bush, though,' he added eagerly.

Flo rolled her eyes and puffed at her fluffy blonde

fringe. 'Just listen!' she demanded. 'We are going to make a Natural History Documentary starting right here. In your house. Now.'

'But . . .' Felix began.

Flo was On A Roll, however.

'Before we go to Africa,' she went on, 'we'll have to Make Do with filming the wildlife around us. It is what other people do. Look at all those cameramen – and *women* –' she added, with emphasis, 'who film all the mice and birds and frogs and whatnot for that *Spring Safari Live* programme on the telly. I bet they really wish they were in Africa filming lions and giraffes and things, but they probably haven't had enough training yet. I s'pect the telly people get them to film frogs and whatnot *first*, and once they have done that enough times, they get to go to Africa. So, it Stands To Reason, that is what we will have to do.'

'You keep saying "we" . . .' Felix tried again, but Flo was already prowling around, looking for things to film with Dad's camera.

'Your dog!' Flo cried, coming across Felix's fat Labrador, who was snoozing on the landing. 'Perfect . . .' And she shoved the camera into Felix's hands and commanded him to 'Press record!'

Then Flo noisily cleared her throat and importantly consulted the clipboard which she had insisted on having 'because I am the Director of this film, and that is what Directors do'.

Felix sighed and trained the camera on Flo and his dog, Dyson.

'Here we have a typical example of the species *Labradorus*, er, *fattifus*,' Flo said. She was leaning forward in a strange, hunched-up way and talking in a whispery voice.

Felix stopped filming. 'Why are you being weird?' he asked.

Flo scowled. 'I am not "being weird",' she said. 'I am talking like all the Professionals do.' She cleared her throat again and gestured to Felix to carry on filming. 'This typical example of *Labradorus fattifus*,' she continued, 'is called Dyson. He lives in a house and lies about all day. In the wild this beast would have to hunt for his food, which would make him less *fattifus* and more *thinnifus*.'

'Sorry,' Felix said, looking around the camera at his dog. 'Flo doesn't mean to be rude, Dyson.'

'Rowf?' Dyson lifted his head at the sound of Felix calling his name and looked hopefully at him, thinking that perhaps 'walkies' or 'food' might be on the agenda.

Flo gave Dyson a stern look, then continued along

4

the landing. Felix noted with dread that she was heading towards his older brother's bedroom.

'And now,' she hissed, glancing furtively around, 'we are going into a particularly dangerous and stinky habitat of Much Smelliness. We shall have to Proceed With Caution to avoid startling the Resident of this Domain.'

'What are you doing now, Flo?' asked Felix anxiously. 'Oh! Watch out!'

Flo had just trodden on something and was tottering backwards, her arms flailing. 'What –?' she cried as she fell.

'MIIIIAAAAOOOOW!' said the 'something' which, it now became clear, was Colin the cat, who had been snoozing in a patch of sunlight on the carpet.

Colin arched his back, his fur standing on end. He hissed and spat at Felix and Flo before streaking down the landing like an angry, furry rocket.

'Quick!' Flo cried, picking herself up off the carpet. 'Record it! This is excellent Filming Material.' She

began scribbling
furiously on her
clipboard.

Felix decided that if he
could not beat Flo, he may
as well join her. He leaped
into action and managed to
catch the scene on film, while
delivering his own excitable commentary in what he
thought was a marvellous Voice-Over Effect.

'An excellent example of the species *Catticus
evillus*!' he exclaimed. 'As you can see, this animal
is very upset at being disturbed from its afternoon
sleep. You can clearly see the sharpness of the
creature's claws and the nastiness of its teeth 'n'
fur 'n' stuff—'

Felix did not get the chance to finish his Voice-
Over Effect, as a hand had come from behind him,
grabbing the camera.

'HEY!' Felix shouted, whirling around to come
face to face with his older brother, Merv, who

was grinning maliciously and pointing the camera directly at Felix.

Flo had managed to melt mysteriously into the wallpaper.

'And here we have the species *Squirticus farticus*,' said Merv, continuing the documentary in his own style. 'An annoying little beast who creeps up on you unawares and is generally found where he is least wanted—'

'Gimme that!' Felix snarled. He made a lunge for his brother. 'You are the only *Farticus* around here! *Farticus maximus*, in fact.'

Merv had the advantage of being quite a bit taller and stronger than poor Felix, so he simply held the camera aloft and left it running in order to capture the full extent of Felix's fury. With his other hand Merv pushed against Felix's head to stop Felix from running at him.

'GrrrrrrRRRR!' said Felix.

'A feisty creature, I'm sure our viewers will agree,' said Merv, raising his voice over his little brother's growling. 'Listen to those noises of aggression.'

'Gimme the camera! You'll break it, you great smelly . . . IDIOT!' Felix shouted.

'Oooh, I am so scared of you,' said Merv, deadpan.

Felix swiped uselessly with both hands as his brother pushed harder on his head.

'What are you up to?' Mum's voice roared.

She appeared at the top of the stairs just as Felix realized he was losing this particular battle. He relaxed ever so slightly and stopped leaning into Merv just at the moment that Merv decided to let him go.

And that is how Felix found himself careering backwards into Mum, who quickly grabbed hold of the banister with one hand and Felix with the other.

'D'OH!' Mum cried. 'Am I glad you two will be on separate continents by the end of the week!' Then she spotted Flo, who was sitting on her haunches in an attempt to make herself look as invisible as possible. 'I might have known *you* would be involved in this commotion, madam,' Mum added. (She was Not That Keen on Flo and quite often called her 'madam'.) 'It's just as well you are not coming to Africa with us.'

'What?' Flo shouted, forgetting she was supposed to be invisible. 'You told me I was coming too, Felix!'

Felix blanched. 'I never!'

'Did too!' Flo protested. All her bossiness had melted away and her bottom lip was now trembling dangerously.

Felix was appalled. He had *never* told Flo that. He had tried to correct her whenever she had said 'when *we* go to Africa', but she had not let him Get A Word In Edgeways!

Merv watched the scene with barely concealed amusement, while Mum rolled her eyes and went back downstairs muttering, 'Here we go again . . .' as Flo became suddenly and rather terrifyingly taller than normal.

She took three strides over to Felix, ignoring Merv who was laughing out loud, and pushed her face up close to him.

'I cannot *believe*,' she said, through gritted teeth,

'that you could even *think* of going to Africa without me, your BEST FRIEND!'

Felix tried to back away but realized he was dangerously near the top of the stairs. 'S-s-sorry, Flo,' he stammered. 'We are only going cos of Dad's business trip and I did try to tell you – Merv is not coming either, cos he's got exams and—'

Flo pushed her face even closer to Felix's and spat her words out so that Felix felt his face get a bit wet. 'Listen, buster,' said Flo in a very mean voice. 'You had better do something about this, or we will NEVER be friends again. Do you understand?'

And with that, she pushed past Felix and ran out of the house crying noisily.

10

CHAPTER 2

BISCUITS AND CONVERSATION

It was true: Felix's dad was going on a business trip to Africa, and he had decided it was a fantastic opportunity for Felix and Mum to come, too.

As Felix had said to Flo, Merv had to stay behind to do his exams, but as he put it, 'I wouldn't want to go on holiday with my fart-face of a little brother anyway,' so that was all right.

Felix was over the moon with happiness: he had wanted to go to Africa ever since he could remember, mainly because he loved animals so much, but also because his uncle Zed had travelled around Africa and had told him so many stories about it.

So when Dad had suggested to Mum, 'Why don't

you take your brother Zed? He could get one of his contacts in Botswana to take you on a safari,' Felix had been *so* over the moon, he felt as if he had turned into a spaceship and been sent zooming out of the Solar System into the farthest part of the Milky Way.

'Yaaaaaay!' Felix had yelled, hurtling around the table at top speed, doing an impression of said spaceship.

'Well done, Ian,' Mum had said darkly. 'We could have had that little chat IN PRIVATE first . . .'

The next day was a Saturday. Felix asked Mum to take him to his uncle's narrowboat so that he could 'hang out and ask questions about Africa'. Zed and his girlfriend Silver knew loads about Africa because of their travels. (Even their narrowboat where they lived was called an African word: *Kiboko*, which is the Swahili word for 'hippo'.)

But although Felix did, of course, want to talk about Africa, he also really wanted to talk about Flo going bananas-doolally when she had discovered that she was not coming to Africa with them.

'What am I going to do about Flo?' he asked his uncle.

'I dunno, man.' Zed shook his head sadly, which set the beads in his long, blond dreads tinkling. 'It's a tricky one. I mean, like, she is your best friend, so I guess it's understandable that she's peeved about missing out on your trip of a lifetime.' He popped a whole chocolate biscuit into his mouth and chewed thoughtfully.

While Zed chewed and thought, Felix took a biscuit too and found himself thinking deeply about how he could not remember a time before Flo Small and he had become Best Friends. It did not matter that she was a girl; she was *so* not like other girls that most of the time Felix did not notice she was a girl at all. She was tough and funny and had the most amazing blonde, mad and curly hair, and she laughed like a hyena. And best of all, she thought that animals were the most Important Thing In

The World. So, naturally, she and Felix got on very well indeed. But the trouble was, she did *not* get on very well with Felix's mum and dad – particularly since the Monkey Incident at Shortfleet Safari Park. Therefore there was never going to be any way in a million years that she was going to be allowed to go on holiday with them.

Felix swallowed the rest of his chocolate biscuit and said, 'I should be feeling the most happiest I have ever felt in my Whole Entire Life, but instead I am worried that when I come back Flo will not be my Best Friend any more.'

'I get what you're saying, dude.' Zed nodded wisely. 'Hey, Silvs!' he called out to his girlfriend. 'Feels here is having girl trouble!'

Felix blushed furiously. 'Don't say that!' he hissed.

Silver had already heard, however, and emerged from the boat's galley, holding two mugs of sweet peppermint tea. 'I'm all ears, Felix,' she said, smiling.

14

Silver was always so kind, and she did totally understand How To Handle Flo, so Felix explained the problem.

'Easy,' said Silver. 'Buy her some cool African jewellery. Works every time,' she added, jingling her armoury of bangles and winking at Zed.

Zed grinned. 'Yeah, man, you can get away with a lot if you buy a girl jewellery.'

Silver stuck out her tongue and they both laughed.

Felix wriggled. 'I don't know. I think Flo would want something much more special than that. Do you have any other ideas?' he added hopefully.

Silver pulled a face. 'Not sure. You'll have to ask Bibi.'

'Who's "B.B."?' said Felix.

'Bibi, man! He's the dude who's going to take us on safari,' said Zed. He handed Felix the biscuit tin again. Zed believed that biscuits were 'an aid to good conversation', which was one of the many, many reasons that Felix loved his uncle so much. 'Not only that,' Zed went on. 'Bibi's the best guy I've ever met, isn't he, Silvs?'

Silver nodded. 'We met him the last time we went to Botswana. Zed has contacted him and asked him to take you around the Moremi Game Reserve. He'll look after you like you're his own family.'

'Yeah,' said Zed. 'And he knows everything there is to know about wildlife. I learned all I know from him,' he added.

Felix had a sneaking suspicion that Zed and Silver were trying to Change The Subject.

'Yeah, so we'll, like, get to go to his village and stay a night at his house,' Zed went on, 'and then he'll take us into a game reserve to look at the animals and birds. Any questions you have – about nature or even special presents for girls –' he broke off and winked at Silver – 'well, let's just say Bibi is your man.'

'Wow, I am sooooooo jealous!' said Silver, with a sigh.

'Can't you come too?' Felix asked her.

'That would be sweet,' said Silver. 'But there's no way your mum could cope with me *and* Zed on holiday.'

'Yeah,' Zed agreed. 'The vibe would make it wrong, man.'

Felix frowned. 'Just don't bring The Vibe then,' he said.

Zed chuckled and ruffled Felix's hair.

'I'm going to stay and look after your brother,' said Silver. 'Someone's got to make sure Merv does some work. And I have to feed Colin and Dyson –

and Hammer the hamster!'

Felix picked up Yin, one of his uncle's cats, and touched its nose with his own. 'Merv never does any work, so good luck with that.

But Hammer certainly needs looking after while Colin is around.'

Yin licked Felix's face gently and purred. Not for the first time, Felix found himself wondering why his cat Colin could not be as cute as his uncle's cats, Yin and Yang.

Zed chuckled as if he could read Felix's mind. 'If you think Colin is bad, you wait till you see his big brothers and sisters in the wild.'

Felix frowned. 'What?'

'Big cats, man! Lions – the kings of Africa!'

Then Zed started on a long story about the first time he had seen a lion in the wild. Felix grinned, sat back with another chocolate biscuit and completely forgot about his problems with Flo.

CHAPTER 3

ON ONE CONDITION

Unfortunately for Felix, Flo did not forget. In fact, she made her feelings very clear indeed at school on Monday morning. She refused to sit next to Felix; she wrote secret notes to the Pink Brigade (aka Millie Hampton and Sophie Disbry); she giggled and whispered; and, worst of all, she ignored Felix at break-time.

'I don't know why I miss playing with her when she is being so nasty,' Felix muttered to himself.

He did know really. It was because Flo was the only person who had ever made school bearable and the only person who knew the difference between a black and a white rhino, or an African and an Indian elephant.

She was also the only person who liked poking around in the dirt with sticks to look for bugs.

Felix took himself off to the far side of the playground and found a stick to poke around with on his own. Usually poking around with a stick made him feel Calm and Peaceful, as he would get lost in looking at the tiny creatures that lived in the soil. But today, even this did not make him feel any better.

Felix sat back on his heels and sighed as he looked up at the world of humans.

I bet ants don't get cross with their Best Friend just because their Best Friend is going to Africa and they can't go with them, he thought.

Suddenly Felix realized that Flo and the Pink Brigade were coming towards him. Before he could move away from his corner of the playground, they had circled him.

Flo exchanged a knowing look with the others, then she stepped forward, with her hands on her hips.

Felix cringed. Much as he missed having Flo as his Best Friend, there was always something to be feared about the hands-on-the-hips pose.

'I have decided to forgive you,' Flo announced.

The Pink Brigade sniggered.

'Oh?' said Felix. He glanced nervously around the group before him.

'Yes,' Flo went on importantly. 'I have decided to forgive you – but ON ONE CONDITION!'

Felix shuddered. 'Hmm?' he said worriedly.

'You have to bring me back Something Very, VERY Special to make up for leaving me behind,' she said.

'Yeah, *special*,' squeaked Sophie Disbry.

'OK. Yeah, course I will,' he said. After all, it couldn't be *that* hard to find a present from Africa, could it? 'Like a special cuddly toy or something?' he asked hopefully.

Flo's face darkened and she opened her mouth to speak, but Millie Hampton had leaned in and cupped her hand to Flo's ear and was now whispering something into it. As she whispered, Flo's face changed from Spiky And Scary to Delighted And Mischievous and she nodded slowly. Then Millie stepped back, looking very pleased with herself indeed.

Flo's smile grew broader and broader until it had developed into a Full-On Grin. Then she said, slowly and ever-so-slightly menacingly, '*I* have just had an excellent idea.'

Millie let out a squeak of protest at this, but Flo gave her a shove, so she shut up.

'Oh yeah?' said Felix, sounding a lot tougher than he felt. (His left leg was actually wobbling, he was feeling so completely un-tough at that moment in time.)

'Oh *yeah*!' said Flo. 'You, Felix Stowe, are going to make up for the fact that you are a useless friend.'

'I am?' said Felix.

'You are,' said Flo. 'D'you remember when we went to Shortfleet Safari Park and you had the stupid idea of trying to capture a monkey and we all got into trouble?'

'Well, actually it was *your* idea and—'

'And d'you remember how the man said that it was stealing because the monkeys belonged to the park?'

Felix nodded sadly. There was no point in interrupting Flo when she was On A Roll.

'Well,' said Flo, with a very self-satisfied smirk, 'this is your chance to make it up to me *twice over*. Number One –' she held up a finger – 'you owe me for that Dreadful Day at Shortfleet when you let all the monkeys into the car . . .'

'But it was *you* who opened the windows!' Felix cried.

'AND Number Two,' Flo spoke over him, 'you owe me for not taking me to Africa. Sooooo –' she paused and exchanged another triumphant look with the Pink Brigade – 'you are going to bring me back a baby monkey.'

'BUT –!' Felix tried to protest.

'No buts,' said Flo, sticking her nose in the air. 'If there's no monkey, then, Felix, there is No Us.'

And with that, she turned on her heel and flounced off.

CHAPTER 4

AFRICA TIME

Felix could hardly believe that he was finally on a plane, away from Flo and her horrible girly friends. For now at least. The past week had been awful, but now the holiday had begun.

He sighed as he rested his forehead against the cool glass of the aeroplane window and stared down at the strange landscape. It was so flat! And so yellow and dry-looking.

Those trees are tiny, he thought. They are like balls of string on sticks; messy and spiky.

The ground was rushing up to greet him, the earth sending up clouds of dust as the plane drew nearer and nearer to its landing spot.

'This is it, Zed!' he said excitedly, nudging his uncle, who had fallen asleep and was drooling on to his T-shirt.

'Wha – oh, maaaan,' Zed groaned. 'Don't you ever sleep?'

'Welcome to my world, little brother,' said Mum, sighing and stretching.

The journey from England had taken a whole night and even then they had not reached their final destination. They had had to change planes in Johannesburg in South Africa, where they waved goodbye to Dad. His meetings were there, but Felix, Zed and Mum were going on to Botswana on a much smaller plane, because that was where Bibi lived.

'How can you sleep?' Felix asked, bouncing up and down in his seat. 'Only,' he added, 'I kind of wish I had slept. This journey is taking HOURS.'

Zed grinned. 'That's what a safari is, man. It means "long journey" in Swahili.'

'Yes, but we're not even ON the safari yet!' Felix whined. 'I have not seen a single animal . . .' He craned his neck to look out of the window again. 'Where *are* all the animals?' he pondered. He hoped that Zed was right and that he *would* see lots of animals. From where he was sitting now, things did not look too promising.

The plane started to judder. Felix gripped the armrests on either side of his seat and sat back as the plane came into land. The passengers erupted into joyous applause. Felix cheered, the bubbles of excitement which had been building up inside him over the long journey bursting out of him in little whoops of happiness.

A man in front turned around and looked over the top of his seat at him. For one split second, Felix thought he might be about to tell him off for whooping, but instead, the man beamed and said, 'Welcome to Botswana, young man!'

Felix, Zed and Mum received an equally warm welcome in the airport building. A tall man (even taller than Zed, Felix noticed) was waiting for them in the Arrivals area.

'Hey! Bibi!' Zed cried, bounding up to him. He did a funny handshake with the man, which seemed to take much longer than normal: first the two men took each other's right hand and shook it once, then they left their thumbs linked and made their arms stick out at right angles. Finally, they grabbed the top of each other's hands and went back into a normal handshake.

It was very complicated-looking, but also quite cool, Felix thought. Maybe it is some kind of secret sign? he wondered. He tried to do it using both his own hands.

The tall man saw him and beamed.

Felix gasped. Those teeth! So white! He bet the dentist gave the man *loads* of stickers for keeping them looking that good.

'*Dumela, Rra,*' the man said, using his country's greeting. 'I am Bibi. And you must be Felix?'

Felix suddenly felt very shy. He nodded and took a small step backwards.

Mum jabbed him lightly, 'Say hello!' she hissed.

'*Dumela, Mma!*' said Bibi, looking at Mum.

Mum's face did something funny: her stiff, tired frown sort of crumpled, then it melted away, leaving her face smoother and pinker than Felix could ever remember seeing it.

'Oh, oh, *dumela, Rra,*' Mum stammered, trying the strange words. They seemed to roll around her mouth awkwardly.

Zed roared with laughter. 'Sweet!' he cried. 'Never thought I'd hear my big sis having a go at the lingo!' He slapped Bibi on the back. 'It's so good to see you again, man. We can't wait to get going, can we Feels?'

Felix nodded again.

'So, let's not waste time. Follow me!' said Bibi. He led them out of the building to a minibus. 'First I am going to take you to my village,' he explained. 'There we will spend the night before going to the Game Reserve. The journey is very long.'

Felix let out a small groan. 'But I thought we were already there!' he said.

Bibi shook his head. 'My homeland is a big country with lots of space. It will take hours to travel to where we want to go. You must be patient. Patience is something you need a lot of on safari.'

'Yeah,' Zed agreed. 'And the best thing about Africa is that people here like to take things sloooowwww.'

'We call it "Africa time",' said Bibi.

Felix frowned. 'Do the clocks go more slowly here then?' he asked.

Bibi and Zed laughed. 'You could say that!' said Zed.

Mum yawned. 'Sounds like the perfect holiday.'

Bibi opened the minibus door and put their luggage in. They clambered into the hot, airless interior. Mum began fanning her face and looking rather uncomfortable.

'I have some advice for you,' said Bibi. 'You will need to drink a lot. My country is a dry country. You come from a wet land. You are not used to the dust and the heat. You will get a headache if you do not drink lots and lots of water.'

'Can I ask – erm, will we be able to stop . . . on the journey?' Mum asked.

Bibi smiled. '*Mma*,' he said, 'that is not a problem. But I can tell you that even if you drink a lot of water, you will probably not need to stop.'

He climbed into the driver's seat and started the engine.

Mum leaned forward nervously. 'And where would we, er, stop – if we needed to?' she asked.

'Oh, anywhere that is safe to do so,' Bibi said over his shoulder. 'We use what is called the "bush toilet".'

'What's that?' Felix asked, confused.

Zed grinned. 'He means that you have to take a pee in the bushes,' he said.

Felix immediately perked up at this piece of news. Why couldn't adults in England be so relaxed? The number of times he had been on a long car journey with Dad and he had been bursting for the loo, and Dad had made him wait and wait until they found a motorway service station . . .

Mum did not seem to be as enthusiastic as Felix about this way of doing things. 'Is it safe?' she asked.

Bibi shrugged. 'Mostly,' he said. 'If you are careful where you put your feet.' He pulled out of the car park.

Mum pursed her lips. 'I think I'll wait until we get to the camp,' she said.

Zed chuckled. 'Hey, sis, what are you expecting at the camp? Four-star service? There's no bathroom in a tent, man!'

'Clive,' said Mum warningly. She only ever used his real name instead of his nickname when she was annoyed with him. 'I hope I am not going to regret bringing you with me.'

'As if, sis,' said Zed, flinging a long arm around his sister and hugging her to him. 'As if!'

CHAPTER 5

CHICKEN IN A BASKET

Felix had never been a patient passenger in the car, but that was because normally car journeys meant whizzing along an English motorway with nothing to see from the window but miles and miles of tarmac and other cars. Felix usually spent the time desperately looking out for some kind of bird or animal so that he could log it in his Wildlife Diary.

'So, Feels,' Zed said quietly, leaning against Felix. 'D'you want me to ask Bibi about getting Flo a special present? He might have an idea.'

Felix tore his eyes away from the window. 'Not yet,' he said.

He felt his stomach lurch: he did not want to

be reminded about Flo because that reminded him about her demanding a baby monkey, and there was no way he could talk to any of the grown-ups about that, not even Zed.

'Sweet,' said Zed, settling himself back into his seat. 'I'm going to have a zizz then,' he sighed.

Mum rolled her eyes. 'Why break the habit of a lifetime?'

Bibi turned his head to join in the conversation. 'You might as well sleep, *Mma*,' he said to Mum. 'It is a long way.'

Felix felt sure that this would become the phrase of the holiday.

He did not mind too much, though. Even in Maun, the town the small airport was in, there was so much to see – Africa was definitely a way cooler place to live than England. For a start there were animals EVERYWHERE. People just carried them around with them wherever they went. There was a woman walking down the road with a shopping basket slung over her arm. When Felix took a closer

look he saw two chickens' heads
peeping out over the edge. For
a moment he thought that
they were chickens which she
had bought to take home to
cook, but then one of them
bobbed its head right up
and squawked loudly! Then
the other one got cross with
the squawky one and tried flapping its wings. The
woman shook the basket irritably and patted the
chickens back down inside.

'Mum . . . Can we have chickens?' Felix asked
when he saw this.

'Don't start!' Mum warned. 'You've asked me that
before – don't you remember what I said?'

'Ye-es,' Felix said with a sigh. 'Colin would eat
them.'

Zed opened one eye and chuckled. 'You've never
been animal-mad, have you, sis?'

Mum just snorted and went back to reading the

guidebook she had brought with her.

'Chickens are very good animals to keep,' said Bibi, glancing back over his shoulder. 'You have your fresh eggs every day, and then you can cook the chicken too,' he pointed out.

Felix shuddered. 'I couldn't eat one of my pets,' he said.

'A chicken is not a pet!' Bibi cried.

'My thoughts exactly,' Mum muttered.

Felix was about to respond when he was distracted by something on the road.

'Wow, look at that!' he shouted, prodding his uncle to get his attention. 'Donkeys! And . . . goats . . . and a cow! In the middle of the road! In town! Just walking – in the middle of the road!'

Bibi grinned. 'This is normal. The people are taking them to market.'

Felix suddenly felt almost sick with envy. English towns were just too neat and tidy. No one ever walked around with live chickens in a shopping basket, and there were certainly no goats, donkeys

or cows on the high street. Felix decided that English towns could learn a lot from African ones.

The roads became dustier and bumpier as Bibi drove into open country. Felix kept his eyes peeled for signs of wildlife. He was not disappointed.

'Wow! What are those?' he cried, sitting up and pointing out of the window.

Bibi glanced over to the left. 'They are warthogs,' he said. 'That is a family group. The male is the one with four warts on its face.'

Felix wished he could get his camera out of the suitcase.

'Do not worry,' said Bibi, as if reading his mind. 'You will see warthogs all over the place. They are not so exciting. In fact, there are annoying. They get into the village sometimes and dig up the vegetables and go through our rubbish.'

'Like the foxes and badgers at home!' said Mum.

Felix could not help thinking that warthogs were a lot more exciting than foxes and badgers. 'What about monkeys?' he asked carelessly. 'Do they ever come into the village?'

Bibi pulled a face in the rear-view mirror. 'They certainly do, the pests!'

'Why are they pests?' Felix asked.

Zed chuckled. 'Remember those monkeys at Shortfleet?'

'I'd rather not,' Mum muttered. '*They* were certainly pests.'

Felix ignored Mum and shuffled forward in his seat. 'Why are monkeys a pest in the wild?'

'No animal is a pest when it sticks to its natural habitat in the wild,' said Bibi. 'It is when animals come into contact with man that the problems begin. Whoooa—!'

He gave a sudden shout and slammed on the brakes as an ostrich ran out in front of the minibus, waving its huge wings threateningly, and arching its long neck.

Bibi hooted the horn and the ostrich turned and ran back

into the bush at the side of the road, hissing and flapping as it went.

Felix bounced up and down in his seat. 'Wow!' he cried. 'This is a lot more exciting than driving around at home! Mum, imagine if an ostrich ran out in front of us on the school run! You would say LOADS more rude words—!'

'That's enough, Felix,' said Mum.

Bibi laughed. 'As I said, it is when animals come into contact with man that the problems begin!'

The journey was soooooooooooo long. Occasionally they passed a small group of mud huts or some more cows, but for ages and ages there was nothing to see but miles and miles of rough, red road, leading seemingly nowhere.

Felix was bored.

'Are we going the right way?' he asked Bibi. 'How do you know which way to drive?'

Bibi grinned at him in the rear-view mirror. 'What are you talking about, Felix?' he teased.

'I have eyes! I use my eyes!'

Felix shook his head. 'I mean, there are no road signs, and all these roads look the same. So how do you know that this is the right way from the airport to your village?'

Bibi was giggling now. 'You are a funny little man,' he said. 'I have lived in this country all my life! I know the roads.'

Felix was not going to let this go, however. 'Yes, but I've lived in my country all of my life and I don't know all the roads, and if some of them look the same and don't have road signs, it's quite easy to get lost. Mum is always getting lost, especially when she has to go anywhere that has roundabouts. And once she got so lost that she started shouting and saying that if the council didn't flipping well—'

'I think what Bibi is trying to say, Felix,' Mum said, leaning forward and giving him another one of her That's-Enough-Now looks, 'is that there are not as many roads here as in England. If you look at the

43

map,' she added, pointing in the guidebook, 'there are only a few main roads.'

Felix wanted to explain that he just couldn't understand how Bibi could tell the difference between one long line of red road and another. There were no landmarks, as far as he could tell – unless you could remember the shape of a tree or the position of a certain type of bush. Everything looked the same forever. The little villages they had passed along the way were all so similar: clusters of small, round huts with thatched roofs, donkeys, goats and cattle wandering around with the people, wire fences enclosing everything. How did Bibi even know which was *his* village when all the houses and the villages looked alike? Maybe if Bibi came to England he would think the same about the streets and houses there? Felix reasoned. But no, in England there were at least street signs.

Suddenly Bibi leaned out of the window and gave a shout as he brought the minibus to a standstill on the edge of yet another group of huts. He was grinning even more broadly, and waving at someone or something ahead. He beeped the horn and Felix realized that a crowd of people were emerging from the trees to the right-hand side.

Bibi cut the engine and Felix heard laughter and shouting and saw people of all ages coming towards the minibus, waving and smiling. Some of them were carrying huge bundles on their heads, without even using their hands to balance them there! Felix was very impressed and decided he would learn how to do this so that he could carry his school books and still have his hands free for doing more important stuff.

'What's going on?' Mum asked. She sounded worried. She muttered something about a 'tourist trap,' which Felix thought did not sound very nice. He knew about animal traps, and he had a nasty vision of himself and his family being put in a cage.

Mum nudged Zed and was urging him to 'ask Bibi why we have stopped in the middle of nowhere'

when Bibi turned to face them and, spreading his arms wide, he said, 'Welcome to my village!'

CHAPTER 6

A NEW FRIEND

No wonder Uncle Zed loved Africa so much.

'I am going to have to come and live here as soon as I am old enough to leave home,' Felix told himself.

He took in the circle of tiny mud huts and the dusty yellow dogs running around; he gazed at the children who sat in shady doorways and the old women who crouched over pots on little stoves. He stared at the goats nibbling idly at the scrubby grass and bushes. He drank it all in and sighed happily.

Then, just as Felix thought things could not possibly get any better, Bibi put two fingers to his mouth and let out the loudest whistle Felix had ever heard. Immediately a face appeared from the furthest hut, and then the body followed, careering towards Bibi at full pelt.

'DADDY!' cried the figure.

Bibi held out his arms to the child and swooped her up in the air, as she giggled and wriggled, crying, 'Put me down! Put me down NOW!'

Bibi set the girl down and then said proudly, 'Everyone, this is my daughter, Harmony. Harmony, say hello to our guests.'

'Hello to our guests!' said Harmony. Then she let out the most extraordinarily loud, hyena-style laugh.

The girl was about the same height as Felix. She had a mischievous look in her eye; her hair was a dark, fluffy cloud that framed her pretty face like a brown halo and was every bit as curly and amazing as Flo's hair.

Felix had always loved Flo's hair: it was so wild. He had often thought what it would be like to touch it. Would it be bouncy? Could you hide things in it? He found himself having the exact same thoughts about this girl's hair, too.

'Harmony,' said Bibi in a warning tone. 'Introduce yourself properly, please.'

The girl rolled her eyes, then she went up to Felix and pumped his hand up and down and expertly twisted it around to hook his thumb with hers in the traditional handshake Bibi had given Zed.

'Hello. What is your name?' she asked.

'I'm Felix,' said Felix, pulling his hand back. It felt as though it had been through a tumble-dryer on fast spin.

'Well, that's good,' said the girl. 'And don't call me Harmony – only my daddy calls me this. You can call me Mo.'

Mum gasped when she heard this and started to say something, but Mo took her by surprise by grasping her hand and giving it the same treatment she had given Felix's. '*Dumela, Mma,*' she said. Then she added, 'Hello, madam,' and batted her eyelashes.

Felix watched Mum nervously. He did not think it had been a good idea for Mo to call Mum 'madam'. Mum called Flo 'madam' when she was cross. Like the time Flo had put Hammer the hamster in the fridge in the lettuce compartment 'because he needed a change of scene'.

However, Mum simply stammered, 'Oh, I'm – call me Marge.'

Soon Zed and Mum were busy chattering away to Bibi about plans for their trip, so Mo slipped aside to talk to Felix.

'Grown-ups are so borrring,' she said. 'Who cares about all that polite chit-chat that they do. Will you be my friend?'

Felix nodded enthusiastically.

'Oh good. Because I have always wanted an English boyfriend.'

'Ah!' Felix was taken aback. 'I – I don't really want to be a *boy*-friend,' he muttered.

Mo frowned and crossed her arms tightly across her chest. 'What are you talking about? Hmmm? You want to be my friend, and you are a boy and you are English. So therefore you can be my English Boy Friend.'

'Oh.' Felix blushed. 'OK,' he said.

He looked at Mo's fierce dark brown eyes and her incredible hair and her shiny dark skin and found himself thinking how cool she was. This made him feel even more timid. He did not know what to say next.

'How come you can speak such good English?' he tried.

Mo roared her hyena-laugh. 'What a silly question! I speak English because I go to school! Don't you go to school to learn things?'

'Well, yes,' Felix admitted. 'Only we don't learn useful things.'

Mo shook her head and puffed at her hair. 'But you can speak English too, so you must have learned *something* right.' Then she put her hands on her hips in a pose that Felix recognized with a shiver of dread. 'Anyway, listen to me, Feeeliiiix,' she said, trying out his name, drawing out each last syllable. 'I can speak three different languages, so you had better be nice to me, or I will go and talk about you behind your back in Setswana or Kalanga and then you will not know what I am talking about!'

Felix sighed. He was used to this kind of thing. Flo was always talking in secret languages to the Pink Brigade when she was fed up with him.

'It's OK,' he said. 'I will be nice to you.'

'Good,' said Mo, with a decisive nod. 'So let's leave the boring grown-ups to it, and I will show you how to stalk a lion and catch it.'

A strong hand appeared on Mo's shoulder, restraining her.

'Oh no you won't, young lady,' said Bibi firmly. 'We are here to look after our guests, not to lead them into danger. Anyway, it is time to eat.'

Zed and Mum were right behind him.

'Y'know, Mo, you like, kind of remind me of someone,' said Zed. 'Do you know what I mean, guys?'

'Don't we just,' muttered Mum. 'Don't we just . . .'

CHAPTER 7

A SPECIAL KIND OF PET

The meal was delicious, even though it was mostly made of vegetables, which Felix was not keen on Under Normal Circumstances. But sitting cross-legged on the floor and eating at a funny, low table (*and being told you had to use your fingers because there were no knives and forks*) seemed to make everything taste a million times better than English food.

Even the thick porridge, which came with the stew, was yummy. Bibi said it was called 'pap' or '*bogobe*'.

'It is made from sorghum wheat, which is our main crop,' he told them. 'We have it with everything.'

He showed them how to eat it by using his fingers

to take a chunk of the thick porridge and scoop the vegetable stew on to the top, before popping the whole lot into his mouth.

After the meal, Mo took Felix by the elbow and led him slowly and quietly away from the table.

'Come with me,' she hissed. 'I have something to show you.'

Felix happily let himself be led away. The grown-ups were poring over maps and talking seriously about the journey to the game reserve. As excited as Felix was about going camping, the details of which roads to take and where they would stop to get food and water were not exactly thrilling.

When Mo said the words 'I have got a pet. Would you like to meet him?', there was really only one response to that.

'Yes *please*!' said Felix. 'I have pets too . . .' he began, feeling at last that there was something they had in common.

'I do not think you will have a pet as good as my pet,' Mo said.

'Oh,' said Felix. Then he thought about his pets, whom he loved, but who were admittedly quite normal and boring sorts of pets. People in Africa probably did not have normal and boring sorts of pets, he realized.

Then Felix had an exciting thought.

Maybe Mo has a baby monkey as a pet! Maybe I could ask her where she got it and then find out how I could get one for Flo?

He followed Mo to the back of the hut where it was cool and dark. She crouched down and started to make a kissing noise – the sort of noise people make when they are trying to get a cat to come out and say hello.

'Kabelo! Come on, Kabelo!' she sang. 'Where are you now?'

Felix sat back on his haunches. 'Is it a monkey?' he asked hopefully.

'No,' said Mo. 'Guess again!' and she made the kissing noise once more.

'A cat?' Felix suggested.

 56

'Tsk!' Mo looked over her shoulder at him and sucked her teeth. 'A *cat*!' she repeated the word as if it was something very nasty indeed. 'What is the use of a cat for a pet? Cats are bad pets. They only look after themselves. Who would want a cat as a pet?'

Felix opened his mouth to protest that, actually, he had a cat called Colin. Then he checked himself. Mo was right: Colin was a useless pet. He was vicious and mean to Dyson the dog, he tried to eat Hammer the hamster all the time, and he only came near Felix when he needed to be fed. When you wanted him you couldn't find him, and when you did come across him he was usually up to no good. So Felix just sighed and waited to see who this 'Kabelo' was.

Suddenly there was a rustling, and a small furry face peered out at the children from the shadows. It had tiny, dark eyes, a pointy little nose and rounded ears. It looked like a cross between a squirrel and a teddy bear, Felix thought. Then he saw the stripy body.

'Oh! It's a banded mongoose!' he cried. 'I've seen them on the telly.' The little creature started at the sound of Felix's voice and scuttled back into the shadows.

Mo seemed surprised and a bit irritated that Felix recognized what kind of animal Kabelo was.

'Now look,' she snapped. 'You have frightened him. You must be quiet. He is not used to strangers. Especially not funny-looking ones, like you.'

She went back to coaxing the animal out, and at last managed to lay her hands on him.

'Here you are,' she said, holding the mongoose out to Felix. 'Felix meet Kabelo, Kabelo meet Felix. I call him "Kabelo" because he was a present to me from my daddy,' she explained, 'and "Kabelo" means "gift" or "given" in Setswana.'

Felix was open-mouthed with amazement. A banded mongoose as a present! Surely this proved that Bibi would be just the right person to ask about getting a monkey for Flo. What a dad Bibi must be, Felix thought. His own dad's idea of a good present was a puncture repair kit for his bike which was 'both practical and unusual as a gift', according to Dad. According to Felix, it was Boring and Disappointing. (There had been a lot of tears and shouting, that particular birthday . . .)

'Can I hold him?' Felix whispered.

'No,' said Mo, clutching the mongoose to her. 'He can bite you and if he does, my daddy will be very cross.'

I think *I* would be very cross too, Felix thought, but something about the look on Mo's face prevented him from saying anything.

'I will bring him in to sit on my lap while we talk,' said Mo. 'You can stroke him while I hold on to him.'

The children went back to the table to sit with the adults.

Bibi was talking about the campsite. 'It will be very comfortable for you,' he was assuring Mum, who had her worried face back on again.

'What happens if, say, a lion comes into the camp?' she asked. She was trying to keep her voice as careless as she could.

'Less stress, sis,' said Zed. 'Bibi knows how to be safe, don't you, man?'

'I have never had a lion come into my camp,' Bibi assured them.

'Daddy! That is not true!' Mo protested. 'What about the time that silly man got up in the night to go to the toilet and a lion jumped out from the bushes and snatched his pants from him and—'

'Harmony!' said Bibi sharply.

'It is important to tell our guests how to be safe around the wildlife,' Mo insisted. 'What about the time you camped by the lake and a hippo left a HUGE pile of poo right outside the—'

'Harmony!' Bibi said, even more sharply. 'That is enough. You will upset our guests.'

 60

Felix was hanging on Mo's every word. 'That's amazing,' he breathed. 'How close was the poo to the tent?'

'RIGHT outside the opening,' said Mo. 'Imagine if the hippo had taken another step backwards.' She got up and started acting out the hippo's movements, lumbering around and pretending that she was about to bump into a tent with her bottom. 'It would have sat right on top of the people in the tent! And probably covered them in poo as well!'

Mo and Felix dissolved into fits of giggles and hyena-laughter.

'I am sorry, *Mma*,' Bibi said to Mum. 'Harmony is rather excited.'

Mum's face had gone green. She clutched at the low table as though to steady herself. 'It's – it's OK . . .' she said.

Suddenly one corner of the table lurched downward, as though someone had chopped one of its legs off. The cups of redbush tea that Bibi had given to Mum and Zed slid towards Felix. He jumped out of the way just in time to avoid being soaked with the scalding liquid.

Mo giggled.

'Oh! I'm so sorry!' Mum cried, thinking it was her fault.

'Whoa!' cried Zed, tipping back on his heels.

'It is my daughter who should be sorry,' Bibi began. He was frowning at Harmony, but she was not near enough to the table to have been responsible. Then it dropped sharply down to the other side and this time Bibi grabbed at it. 'Harmony!' he admonished. 'Have you brought Kabelo in here again? I have told you not to bring him when we have guests.'

'What's happening, man?' asked Zed, scrabbling to get up. He reached forward to stop the maps falling on to the floor.

The table was shaking and juddering now. Mum was looking greener than ever.

'It's not a . . . an earthquake, is it?' she whispered, clutching on to Zed, who put his arm around her.

Mo laughed. 'An *earthquake*!' she scoffed.

Bibi frowned. 'Catch him and take him away,' he demanded. Then he turned apologetically to Mum and Zed. 'I am sorry,' he said. 'Harmony has a pet mongoose and I am afraid that he likes to dig for bugs in the sand. I have told her so many times not to let him into the hut. He ruins the floor! Mongoose like to dig at the base of tree trunks,' he went on, 'so this is why Kabelo likes to do this around the table. He thinks it is a tree. He really is a stupid and annoying creature.'

'Daddy!' Mo protested. 'Do not be unkind to my Kabelo!'

'Well, if you listened to your daddy and did not let him into my house, then I would not be unkind,' Bibi said. 'When I gave him to you, I said he had to live outside, but do you listen to me?'

Zed was chuckling. Even Mum was smiling now.

'At least your pets don't dig holes in the carpet!' Mum said to Felix. 'I will have to think twice before complaining about Colin again.'

Felix was not really listening.

Bibi had got Mo a pet mongoose. Surely he could be persuaded to get Felix a pet monkey? He decided to ask Mo about this at the next available opportunity – as soon as he was out of Mum's earshot.

CHAPTER 8

ELE-FANTASTIC!

The whole of the next day was spent travelling across very rough country to the Moremi Game Reserve, where the campsite was. Luckily, for once, Felix slept for most of the journey.

He awoke to the most beautiful sight he had ever seen.

'Elephants!' he cried, sitting bolt upright.

Elephants under the trees, elephants lumbering between the three large tents that were dotted about the clearing, elephants reaching up with their trunks to pluck fruit and lazily crunch on them in the golden light. Elephants: beautiful, majestic, glorious elephants, roaming wild and free.

Felix reached for the video camera which he had asked Mum to get out of the suitcase for him that morning. He felt his throat tighten and thought he might actually cry with happiness.

'We must be very still and very quiet,' said Bibi in hushed tones, as he unloaded the minibus.

'Yes,' said Mo. 'The elephant does not have good

eyesight. She has very good hearing, though.'

'What happens if she hears us?' Felix asked.

'If she hears you and cannot see you clearly,' said Bibi, 'she may get frightened and that is when she may charge.'

'How much, man?' Zed joked. 'I hope she's not too expensive.' He winked at Mo and Felix.

'Oh shut up, Clive,' Mum muttered. 'I refuse to share a tent with you if you insist on telling jokes like that all holiday.'

Mo giggled. 'Your uncle is a funny man,' she said.

Felix was not listening to his mum and uncle bickering. He was drinking in the sight before him. He stopped filming for a second, turned to Bibi and whispered, 'What is the fruit called that they are eating?'

'It is their favourite food,' Bibi explained. 'They will do anything to get hold of it – even walk right into a human encampment, as you can see. It is called "marula". For elephant, the fruit of the marula tree is like a sweet to them. It is a treat, something they cannot get enough of. But it can have a bad effect on them.'

'What's that?' asked Felix.

'They go a bit crazy, like this,' said Mo. She began staggering around and rolling her eyes, letting her tongue loll out of her mouth, and waving an arm in front of her like a lazy elephant's trunk. 'It makes them alllll sleeeepy!' she slurred.

Mum watched Mo's behaviour with one eyebrow raised. 'I think my dear brother might be partial to a bit of the old marula. Have you got a secret stash on your boat, Clive?'

Zed grinned. 'I wish!'

'Alll sleepy, like thiiiisss,' said Mo, enjoying her audience.

'Not so much noise,' said Bibi.

'Ooooo-oo-oooo! Aaaah-ah-ah!'

'Harmony!'

Mo stopped fooling around and looked hurt. 'That was not me, Daddy,' she said. She looked up into the marula trees.

Everyone followed her gaze. There was nothing
to be seen, however, beyond the dark green leaves
and the round yellow fruit, hanging in small clusters.
Suddenly one of the fruit came hurtling out of the
tree and landed close to Mo's feet, making her jump.
She squealed, as did Mum.

Zed and Bibi laughed, while Felix watched the
whole scene in wonder.

'Monkeys!' said Bibi.

Mo rolled her eyes. 'Silly things,' she said, and
grabbed Felix by the hand. 'Come with me. I will
show you around the camp.'

'Will the children be all right?' Mum asked.

'They will be fine,' said Bibi. 'Harmony knows the
rules.'

'But does she know to keep them?' Mum
muttered.

'Hey, look out for the monkeys, man!' Zed
chortled.

I certainly will! thought Felix, as he followed Mo
into the camp.

CHAPTER 9

AFRICAN MAGIC

Felix thought the campsite must be the most heavenly place in the world. It was certainly unlike any campsite he had ever seen or heard of. The only camping he had done before had been with Uncle Zed by the seaside. They had pitched a small two-man tent on a campsite overlooking the beach and had laid out their sleeping bags side by side on mats. The best things about camping had been using the 'outdoors' as a loo, and cooking beans and bacon on a camp stove in front of the tent.

The campsite on the game reserve, however, was Totally Luxurious compared with the one Felix had stayed on with Zed.

70

Mo began her tour by taking Felix around the back of the minibus where a fire had been lit in a big pit in the ground, and a large cauldron of water was hanging on poles over the fire. Next to this was a small folding table on which was a pile of potatoes and a mound of potato peelings. A wonderful smell was coming from another pot sitting on a small stove, and a tall man was bent over the table, peeling

a potato with a small knife. He looked up and grinned, raising the potato in greeting.

'My daddy and I do the cooking with our friend, Elvis. Say hi to Elvis!' said Mo.

'Hi, Elvis!' Felix said shyly.

'*Dumela, Rra!*' said Elvis. 'I hope you are hungry.'

'Yes, very,' Felix answered. His stomach rumbled in agreement. He realized he had not eaten anything for hours. He looked at the pots bubbling away, and was about to ask when supper was when Mo grabbed his arm and pulled him away.

'So, this is the kitchen; that is the food. Boring, boring. Now I will show you the rest of the camp,' said Mo.

'If you think that kitchen is boring, you should see ours at home!' Felix told her. This one was so much better than his own, where you had to wipe down the surfaces and tidy everything into cupboards.

Mo tugged at him impatiently and said something really fast in Setswana to Elvis, adding, 'Come ON, Felix,' to get him moving.

'Er, Mo . . . why is that man called Elvis?' Felix whispered as they left him to his potato-peeling.

Mo looked at him curiously. 'He is called Elvis because that is his name, of course,' she said.

Felix frowned. 'But, well, it's not an African name, is it?'

Mo tutted. 'It is a name that people like. Do you like your name?'

'I – I suppose so,' Felix said. He had not given it much thought.

'And is it English?'

'I don't know. I've never asked anyone,' Felix admitted.

'So,' said Mo, as if that settled the matter.

Felix followed her to where some hammocks were tied up in the trees.

'Oh COOL!' he said. 'I wish we could sleep in these,' he added wistfully.

'Not you,' said Mo. 'You are a tourist so you get to sleep in the fantastic tents with the beds and the mattresses.' She pointed over to the large tents around which the elephants were still standing.

'Oh,' said Felix. 'Isn't it a bit dangerous sleeping here, what with the elephants and everything?'

'The elephants will go away later,' Mo said. 'And the tents are better for people who are not used to living in the wild like I am,' she added proudly.

Felix had a sneaking suspicion that Mo was showing off.

'This is the dining area,' Mo said, gesturing to a canopy in the centre of the camp. 'We call it "The Mess",' Mo went on. 'Here is where you will eat the food that Daddy, Elvis and I will cook for you. Also, it gets very hot in the afternoon, so if you want to get out of the heat, you can sit here in the shade and have a rest – if you don't want to go into the tent.'

Under the canopy was a large table and some

74

camping chairs made from canvas and metal. Felix felt a warm glow settle in the pit of his stomach as he imagined sitting under the canopy watching the elephants while he ate a meal. He planned to film the elephants to make the Best Natural History Documentary Ever. Flo would be so impressed.

Thinking of Flo reminded Felix . . .

'Mo, you know that monkey that threw a fruit at you?' he began. 'And you know your dad gave you Kabelo as a present? Well, I was wondering—'

He stopped abruptly as he saw Mum making her way over to them, grinning.

'Isn't this *wonderful*, Felix?' she said. 'It's much more glamorous than I thought it would be! I'd imagined a tiny little tent in the middle of nowhere with a camping stove and not much more besides. But there are REAL loos AND showers!' she finished happily.

Zed was standing beside her, not looking so happy. 'Man,' he said shaking his head, 'this is not camping for real, is it?'

Felix couldn't help thinking his uncle had a point there.

'I mean, like, when you camp, you are supposed to commune with nature, right?' Zed went on. 'This is like some kind of hotel, dude! I don't want Bibi cooking for me – I want to do the cooking myself! A bathroom in the middle of the bush? Dude, it's just not right. The last time I went on safari, it was not like this.'

'Oh for goodness sake,' said Mum. 'Just shut up and be happy that your sister is not going to moan about roughing it.' She grinned and threw a mock punch at Uncle Zed.

He immediately raised his hands in surrender and shouted, 'Make peace, sis, not war!' then he dived for Mum and tickled her until she begged for mercy.

Mo shook her head. 'What strange people you are,' she said.

Felix nodded. 'You're telling me.' He could not help smiling, though. He had never seen Mum look so happy and relaxed.

African magic, he thought to himself. If only I could take some of that home to Flo. Maybe she would chill out and be my Best Friend again.

CHAPTER 10

SPIDERS AND SNAKES

Supper was served early. The sun had already fallen out of the sky like a large orange beach ball, dropped from a great height. It was still warm enough to sit outside, so everyone gathered around the table under the canopy. Bibi chatted to them about the safari as they lapped up another delicious meal. This time they had to sit on chairs and eat with knives and forks, much to Felix's disappointment, but it was a small price to pay for eating outside with the noises of the African bush in the background.

Bibi talked between mouthfuls. 'We eat early because we go to bed early,' he explained. 'And can you guess why?'

'Because you are hungry and tired?' Felix offered.

Mo tutted. 'Because we get up early too!' she said.

'Great!' said Felix. 'I love getting up early.'

Mum groaned softly. 'How early is early?' she asked. 'In the morning, I mean.'

Bibi beamed. 'Five o'clock,' he said.

Mum's eyes bulged. 'What?' she cried. 'I thought this was supposed to be a holiday!'

'Less stress, sis,' said Zed. 'It's best to go out early – you see the most animals, and it's not so hot. No point in going out in the heat. If it's too hot for humans, it's too hot for animals.'

'That is right. Now, there are a few rules that I must talk to you about, young man,' said Bibi.

Mo pulled a face at Felix so that her dad couldn't see.

Bibi went on. 'You should know that even though this camp is very luxurious and is made to be a "home from home" for you, you are still very much out in the wild. And this means that you need to respect nature.'

'Oh, man!' said Zed. 'Felix knows all about respecting nature, don't you, Feels?'

Felix nodded enthusiastically. 'I LOVE nature!' he said.

'That is very good. But I still have to tell you these things for your own safety. You must remember that the animals in my country are very different from the animals where you come from. You must keep your tents shut at *all times* when you are away from them. Actually it is probably better if you keep them shut when you are in them too.'

Mum immediately looked panicky. 'This is exactly what I was afraid of! It's snakes, isn't it? I think I might have to sleep in the bus.'

'No, no!' said Bibi. 'It is the monkeys you must be careful of.'

Felix pricked up his ears.

'They can be very naughty' Bibi went on, 'as I told you in my village. They are inquisitive animals.'

'But what about spiders?' Mum was asking.
'I cannot *stand* them. What if they are lying in wait

 80

in the grass, ready to pounce into the tent when I
open it!'

Felix was a little embarrassed at Mum's silly
comments. 'Mum! Spiders do not pounce on people!
They eat flies and things. And snakes do not attack
people either unless they are trapped or frightened,
actually. In fact, I have read in my *Big Book of Safari
Facts* about how they really do get their prey. Snakes
like to hide in wait
and—'

'Man,' Zed said in a
warning tone. 'Don't
mention snakes. Your
mum's already anxious
enough as it is, dude.'

'Please, do not
worry,' Bibi said.
'Felix is right. Snakes and spiders are very shy – the
poisonous ones especially so. They mostly only use
their poison on a human when they are cornered.
You will not see anything bad when you are on safari

with me. I will take good care of you.'

'Bibi's right,' said Zed. 'When Silvs and I lived here we never saw anything like that. The only way you would get freaked out by a spider or snake is if you went poking about in long grass or in a hole or something and you scared them.'

Mo had been listening to this exchange with interest. 'That is not completely true though, is it, Daddy? What about the time that Grandmother was driving to Johannesburg to sell those clothes at the market? She was driving very fast along the main road and she heard a hissing noise,' Mo said, her eyes shining as she got into her story. 'She thought to herself, "I must stop the car to see if I am getting a flat tyre," and as she pulled over, a snake that had been hiding in the warm car leaped up in her face and—'

'Harmony!' Bibi cried, shaking his head at his daughter. 'Stop now.'

'Yeah, that's right,' Zed chipped in excitedly, seeming to forget his advice to Felix. 'I remember

 82

you told me that the snake bit her on the ankle before she even knew it was in the car, didn't you, man?'

Mum let out a strangled whimper.

Bibi groaned and put his head in his hands. 'Really, this is not a good story to tell *Mma*,' he said.

Zed jumped up, slapping his thigh and said, 'Well, enough talking, eh? Let's hit the sack. The sooner we get to sleep, the sooner we can get up and get going, man! I'll just nip to the bathroom . . .'

He loped off in the direction of the shower block, leaving Bibi to console Mum with reassuring words about how what had happened to his mother had been a one-off and that he personally would check the tents and the safari jeep for anything dangerous.

'OK,' Mum said eventually. 'I am sure we will be safe in your hands, Bibi.' She pushed back her chair and made to leave the table. But as she did this, Zed came running back from the shower block.

'Arghhhhh!' He was waving his hands around

and jabbering wildly. 'SPIDER! SPIDER! BIG, FAT, HAIRY—!'

'No!' cried Bibi in disbelief.

Felix's heart sank. Surely not? This must be Zed's idea of a joke. He could see that Mum had gone as white as a ghost, even in the light from the campfire. Why did this have to happen on their first night in the wild? Mum would make Bibi drive them to a hotel now. They would be on the road all night . . .

But then Mo burst out laughing. 'Did you not like my present, Mr Zed?' she said.

'Wha—?'

'Harmony,' said Bibi hastily, 'you had better come with me.' He took his daughter firmly by the elbow and dragged her away from the table. Then he made her stand straight in front of him and look him in the eye while he bent low and spoke directly into her face.

Felix could hear Bibi talking to Mo in a tone of voice he recognized, even if he could not understand the language used. When he also saw the look on Mo's face he knew that she was being well and truly told off. Eventually Bibi straightened up and said in English, 'Go and get it.'

Mo scampered into the shower block, pausing only to turn and stick her tongue out at her father the minute he turned his back.

'I am sorry,' said Bibi. 'This is the first time I have let her come away with guests from England. She is showing off, I am afraid. I am sure little girls in England are not like this.' He shook his head sorrowfully.

'Oh don't worry,' said Mum. 'I can assure you they are.' And she shot Felix a knowing look.

Felix was not certain, but he thought Mum might

have been thinking about Flo. If she was, he thought
that was pretty unfair actually, as Flo had never
played a trick like that on anyone. It wasn't that
she was frightened of spiders (she wasn't); she just
didn't think of doing things like that. She was more
likely to tell a tall story about one than hiding one
somewhere as a joke.

Mo came skipping back, holding something in her
hands.

'It is all right, Mr Zed,' she said. 'This is not a
poisonous spider – as you can see I am holding it in
my hands and I am fine!'

'Y-yeah.' Zed faltered, staggering backwards.

'Come and say hello,' Mo said to Felix.

Bibi nodded. 'I promise it won't bite. Harmony
has told me what kind of spider it is. It is safe.
And if you love nature like you say, you should be
interested in this.'

Felix shivered slightly, but he was determined
not to look scared in front of Mo. Also, he secretly
thought Zed was possibly being a bit of a wuss, and

 86

he wanted to prove that he could be braver than his uncle. So he approached Mo cautiously.

Mo slowly opened her hands. Felix held his breath and leaned in as far as he dared to take a look. He was not prepared for what he saw, though, and gasped, leaping backwards.

'Oh!' he cried.

The spider was huge and hairy, with what looked like blue jaws, which seemed quite snappy, and it had four bulging black eyes. It took one look at Felix and bounded out of Mo's hands, and then scuttled off into the darkness.

Mo clapped her hands and roared with laughter. 'That is an African

jumping spider!' she announced.

'You don't say,' muttered Mum.

'It is also completely harmless and not normally to be found sitting on a *toilet seat*,' said Bibi, glowering at his daughter.

'Heeheehee!' Mo was clutching her belly now, her face creased up with laughter.

'OK, man,' said Zed, chuckling nervously. 'I guess that was a pretty neat joke.'

'Well, a joke is a joke,' said Bibi. 'But I do not want any more jokes with spiders while we are camping, Harmony. Do you understand?'

Mo bit her lip to stop herself from laughing. 'OK, Daddy,' she said, nodding her agreement. 'No more jokes with spiders, I promise.'

Felix watched Mo's face carefully.

He could swear that she winked at him very quickly as she said those last words, although it could have been a trick of the firelight, flickering across her face.

CHAPTER 11

CHEEKY MONKEYS

Felix woke to a chorus of chirping, cawing, cackling and croaking. It was pitch dark in the tent, so he thought it must still be night time. Why were all the animals making so much noise outside in the middle of the night?

He leaned over the edge of his camp bed and quietly felt around in his small rucksack for his head torch. Once he had found it, he turned it on and cupped it with one hand so the light did not shine on Mum and Zed and wake them. He looked at his watch.

4.45 a.m. Felix's heart leaped. Bibi had said they needed to be up at 5.00 a.m. for some breakfast before going on their first drive out into the bush.

But he was not sure he wanted to go outside in the dark, particularly after what Bibi had said just before they all turned in the night before.

'There are two rules at night,' he had told them. 'Rule Number One: if you need to pee, you must do so outside, and very close to your tent. If you need to go to the bathroom for anything else –' at this, Mo had sniggered and nudged Felix – 'then you must take a torch and wake someone to go with you to the shower block. I cannot guarantee your safety if you go alone . . . listen!' He had suddenly cupped one hand to his ear.

A low, grumbling sound could just be heard, somewhere out in the darkness.

'Lion!' Mo had breathed, her eyes shining in the firelight.

'Yes, a *long* way away,' Bibi had emphasized, 'but still, we must take precautions. Elvis and I will keep the fire burning all night, just to be sure.'

Felix had gone to bed so excited at the thought of lions prowling around in the black night that he

90

had been convinced he would not sleep. Yet he must
have fallen asleep immediately, as the last thing he
remembered was Mum saying, 'Don't forget what
Bibi said . . .' and after that, nothing.

Now he lay as still as a cat in his sleeping bag and
tried to breathe shallowly so that he could listen to
all the sounds outside.

BOOM!

Something landed on the tent above Felix's head, making the canvas shudder. Felix jumped, his heart banging in his chest.

BOOM! BOOM-DE-BOOM!

Three other somethings landed on the roof and seemed to slide down the walls of the tent. There was a short, sharp cackling, then a patter of feet.

Felix waited to see if there would be any more bumps from above, but no more came, so he let out the breath he had been holding. He was just thinking of swinging his legs over the side of his camp bed and going to wake Zed when there was a harsh call which sounded like someone shouting, 'Go away! Go away!' Felix shivered. Maybe the banging above his head had been some animals landing on the tent and maybe now someone was being attacked by a wild animal right here in the camp! His heart began hammering in his chest again . . .

'Felix!'

'Oh!' he sat bolt upright at the sound of his name from outside the tent flaps.

'It is me. Mo,' said the voice in a harsh whisper.

Felix clambered out of his sleeping bag and hurried to the tent door, which was already open. How had Mo opened it without him hearing? The zip had been so loud last night.

Felix cautiously stuck his head through the gap. 'Hello, Mo. Are you OK? I heard a voice saying "Go away" just now. Was that you?'

Mo chuckled. 'You are a funny boy,' she said. 'That was the Go-Away Bird, of course.'

'What?' Felix was puzzled. What tall story was Mo telling now?

'The Go-Away Bird,' Mo repeated impatiently. 'It is another name for the Grey Lourie, because that is the sound that it makes. You are to come out right now, Felix. Daddy has made some breakfast. We need to get going.'

'OK, I'm coming,' he whispered to Mo.

Felix swung his head torch round to Mum who was stirring and making little grunting noises.

'Whassat?' Mum mumbled grumpily. She propped

93

herself up on one elbow and squinted into the
torchlight.

'Sorry, Mum,' said Felix. 'It's time to get up. I'm
going to get some breakfast.'

'Mugdfgfg,' said Mum and turned over in her
sleeping bag.

Zed let out a humungous snore, and Mum
grunted again.

Felix sighed. He could not understand why the
grown-ups were not leaping out of bed. They were
going on a Real Life Safari, for goodness sake!

Bibi was standing by the fire as Felix emerged
from the tent. He saw a golden glow coming from
the fire, and also light was coming from behind
the tents. Felix turned and gasped. The sun was
appearing over the edge of the horizon, in a semi-
circle of flames, mirroring the campfire. Felix
looked up and saw that above him the sky was
still dark. He could still make out thousands and
thousands of stars in the inky-blue sky, in spite of
the sun rising before him. He looked back at the

sun and saw it had already risen a little further.

He peered back at his tent. He thought he saw some movement, but he could not be certain in the half-light. What had been jumping on it earlier? Was it Mo, mucking about? It couldn't have been that Go-Away Bird, could it? Or lion cubs? But lions didn't climb trees, he was pretty certain of that . . .

Bibi broke into his thoughts, putting a warm hand on his shoulder. 'The sun appears to set and rise fast here, because we are near the equator,' he explained. 'Now come and have some hot chocolate or some redbush tea to warm you. The mornings are cold.'

Felix followed Bibi gratefully to the fire. It certainly was chilly. The night before he had been too hot in his sleeping bag and had lain on top of it, but during the night he had had to sneak into it as the temperature had fallen.

Mo was full of energy, rushing around finding plates and mugs and chattering wildly about the day's plans.

'We are going to have a proper breakfast later,' she said. 'Can you wake your lazybones of a mother and that snoring uncle of yours? We must get on the road, mustn't we, Daddy?'

'Well, I am sorry to have held you all up,' said Mum. 'I've been looking for my hat and sunglasses. I can't seem to find them.'

Mo sniggered. 'You do not need your sunglasses! It is dark!'

'I might need them later . . .' Mum muttered.

'Hey, sorry about the snoring, dude,' said Zed, who was following close behind. He had a serious bed-head: his long, snaky blond hair seemed to have a life of its own this morning, and his face looked a bit crinkled, like a scrunched-up crisp packet. He rubbed his cheeks, yawned and stretched. 'Oh, man, a campfire breakfast! This is the life. Hey, did you hear that banging on the tent earlier, Feels?'

'Yes,' Felix said, grateful his uncle had brought up the subject. 'What do you think it was?'

Zed shrugged. 'Dunno, but whatever it was, they

 96

came back after you got up – jumping and sliding and cackling.'

Bibi took a slurp of his hot, sweet tea and said, 'Monkeys again, probably.'

Mo nodded. 'Oh, yes. I saw them before I came to wake you. They are always doing this: jumping out of the trees and on to the tents. They think the tents are there for them – like our slide in the school playground,' she added with a grin.

'Oh!' said Felix. He wished now that he had been brave enough to get outside the tent to take a look. 'Mo,' he said, sidling up to her so that the adults could not hear, 'I need to ask you about the monkeys—'

'Time to go,' Bibi said suddenly. He kicked earth over the flames of the campfire. 'Mo will stay here with Elvis. We will come back in the middle of the morning and you can have showers and a second, proper breakfast then.'

Felix was disappointed that Mo wouldn't be coming too. Still, he couldn't stay disappointed for long: up at dawn with monkeys jumping on your tent and birds chattering all around you; toast by a campfire and a grown-up telling you there would be a second breakfast later in the morning . . . How could anyone be anything but one hundred and ten per cent happy, living this sort of life?

Bibi loaded some boxes and large plastic containers of water into the special safari jeep, which Elvis had driven to the camp ahead of them. Then, urging them to grab jumpers and blankets, he told everyone to get on board.

'We are going to try and find some lion,' he said. 'So keep your eyes open. If you see anything, tell me and I will stop.'

Mo waved as they climbed in – Mum in the back, Zed and Felix in the middle behind Bibi. The sides of the jeep were open, 'So that you can see the animals clearly,' Bibi told them.

'Why can't you come too?' Felix called out to Mo.

She shook her head and pulled a face. 'Because my daddy has set me some schoolwork to do. And I must help Elvis,' she said, quickly sticking her tongue out once Bibi's back was turned.

'What a shame,' said Mum quietly.

'Yes, it is,' said Felix. 'See you later then.' He shivered. His legs were cold in his shorts.

'Here, man,' said Zed. 'Snuggle up next to me.' He pulled a light woollen blanket from the back of the jeep and laid it over their legs, putting his arm around his nephew.

Using his own language, Bibi called out what could have been a list of instructions to Elvis and Mo. Then he started up the jeep and pulled away from the camp and out, into the bush.

CHAPTER 12

JUST LION AROUND . . .

Felix rested his head in the crook of Zed's arm and closed his eyes for a second so that he could soak up the sounds and smells around him. The inside of his nose felt dry; from breathing in all the dust, he supposed. There was another smell in the air: a kind of refreshing, lemony tang, and faint animal odours too, which reminded him of the smell of the horse dung which was sometimes left behind in the middle of the road at home.

'Bibi.' He leaned forward. 'What is that lemon-type smell?'

Bibi shouted above the noise of the engine. 'It is sage,' he said.

'Yum,' said Zed. 'Sage and onion – delicious!'

Bibi laughed. 'No, we do not eat this type of sage! It is used for keeping the mosquitoes away in traditional medicine.'

Felix thought this sounded like an excellent idea. 'Wow! Can we stop and pick some? We could use it instead of those disgusting pills Mum's making us take.'

Mum leaned over from her seat in the back. 'No way!' she said. 'No disrespect, Bibi,' she added hastily. 'But we are not used to African mosquitoes. I would prefer it if you took the medicine, Felix.'

'Yeah, Feels,' Zed added. 'Your mum is right.'

'Ooh,' Felix slumped back against his uncle.

'You must listen to your mother,' said Bibi. 'Here, we use both traditional and modern medicine.'

Suddenly there was a tremendous riot of cackling in front of the jeep. Bibi swung the steering wheel to the right and came to a stop. 'Guinea fowl!' he exclaimed.

'Look!' Zed pointed at the cluster of birds ahead. Their plumage was dark grey, speckled with lighter grey spots and their heads were a bright red and blue.

Felix immediately reached for his camera. 'Why are the birds making so much noise?' he asked, as he focused on them.

'Because of us, I'd expect,' said Mum.

'No, no, this is exciting, man!' said Zed. 'Guinea fowl kick up a fuss like that when there's lions around . . . "lion around", get it? Lions, "lion" around – lying around!'

Mum snarled like a lion herself. 'Yes, Clive,' she said. 'We get it. It's just not that funny.'

Bibi turned. 'Zed is right. Guinea fowl are very good guards. They will tell you if any big cat is in the area,' he said. 'People sometimes keep them in the villages to protect their chickens from dogs and jackals too.'

Felix's face lit up. 'Can you get guinea fowl in England?' he asked Zed.

His uncle nodded. 'Yeah. My mate Piggy had some to protect his chickens from foxes.'

Mum could see where this was heading and interrupted quickly, 'Felix, I have told you before – we are *not* having chickens, and we are CERTAINLY not having guinea fowl. We have enough animals.'

'What animals do you have, Felix?' Bibi asked him kindly.

Felix replied solemnly, 'I have a dog and a cat and a hamster and I did have a goldfish before someone flushed him down the loo – it wasn't me,' he added quickly.

Bibi chuckled, then he said, 'Ah, but it is good to have a dog. I once had a puppy which I loved very much. He saved my life, but he did not manage to save himself.' He looked suddenly very sad.

Zed sighed heavily. 'Oh, man, I remember that story.'

'Tell me!' said Felix.

Bibi glanced quickly at Zed. 'I don't know . . .'

'Pur-leeeeese!' Felix pleaded.

'It is a very sad story, little dude,' Zed warned him. 'You have to realize life is tough here in Africa.'

'Yes,' said Bibi. 'Please remember this was a matter of life and death. I had no choice . . .'

'OK,' Felix promised.

Bibi began, 'I was on my way to school in my canoe—'

'You canoed to school?' Felix cut in. 'Wow! Mum, can we—?'

'No!' Mum laughed.

'But Mum, we could go along the canal!'

Zed nodded. 'A great way to put Green before the Machine, sis,' he said. 'I'm always telling you driving is bad for the environment.'

'Why don't we let Bibi finish his story?' said Mum.

'You might be put off canoeing for life,' Bibi said. 'I had to canoe to school – it was the only way. I used to take my puppy with me . . .'

Felix gasped with delight.

Then Bibi said, 'One day, I saw something floating in the water. It seemed to be coming closer and closer and I realized it was a crocodile! Well, Felix, what would you have done?'

Felix, wide-eyed, said, 'I would have paddled as fast as I could to get to the other side.'

Bibi shook his head. 'Not possible. The crocodile swims so much faster than a boy can paddle. So, any more ideas? I will give you a clue. Either both myself and the puppy could get eaten by the crocodile, or . . .'

Mum groaned. 'No! You didn't?'

Felix suddenly understood. 'You – you threw the puppy to the crocodile?' he said, his voice small.

Bibi nodded. 'It was the saddest thing I have ever done. But imagine how sad my parents would have been to lose me *and* the puppy? This way, only one of us was sacrificed. This is what life is like in Africa, Felix. It can be hard.'

Felix's throat was dry. He could not think of anything to say.

Zed put his arm around him and gave him a squeeze.

Bibi hastily turned his attention back to the road and said, 'I think we should see what the guinea fowl were warning us about, don't you?'

He drove on, causing the birds to scatter from the path. The jeep went careering through the scrubby landscape, jolting and jarring over dips and ruts in the ground.

'Safari Rule Number One,' said Bibi. 'Do not leave the road.'

He immediately swerved off the road and into the bush.

'Whooah!' Mum shouted, as she was thrown to left and right. 'What's happening?'

Bibi looked over his shoulder and grinned. 'Safari Rule Number Two – ignore Rule Number One!' he cried, stepping on the accelerator.

'I-I d-don't like thiiiis,' Mum said. Her voice wobbled in time to the shaking of the vehicle and her face was white. 'Clive, ask him to stop!'

But as soon as she said this, Bibi braked and slowed right down, saying, 'Lion tracks! Shhh!'

Felix thought it was a bit silly being told to 'shh' when the jeep engine was making so much noise, but then something occurred to him. 'We're not being ch-chased by l-lions, are we?' His voice sounded bumpy too.

'WHA-AT?' Mum cried.

Bibi called back. 'Do not worry, *Mma*. It is we who are doing the chasing – look down and you will see tracks going away from us. At this time of day, the

lions will be hunting – for animals, not humans,' he
added hastily.

Felix tried to look over the side of the jeep, but he
was not sure what lion tracks would look like in this
dusty earth. How could Bibi have spotted them while
driving along? He added this to his ever-lengthening
Mental List of things he wanted to ask about later.

Bibi began driving again, but more carefully
this time.

'Lean in, dude,' Zed whispered into Felix's ear.

'Why?' Felix asked. 'Would a lion jump on top
of me?'

'Ooohh,' Mum quavered.

'No, no. I meant cos of the sharp thorns on some
of these bushes,' Zed said, hugging Felix into him
a little more tightly. 'Don't be scared, sis,' he added
to Mum. 'Bibi wouldn't take us into danger. Just do
what he says and everything will be sweet.'

That's when Felix saw them: two lionesses with
four – no, six! – cubs.

This is more than 'sweet', he thought, as wonder

rose up from his belly and squeezed his chest. This is magic! He trained the camera on them.

'Oh, man!' breathed Zed.

Bibi brought the jeep to a standstill. Then he turned to his passengers and beamed. 'I will leave the engine turning over. The lions see us as one big animal. As long as we stay in the jeep, we are safe. We can get away fast, if we need to.'

Felix filmed the cubs rolling around and playing like kittens. The lionesses stared back at Felix,

gazing right into the camera, lazily flicking their tails and occasionally yawning, showing off huge powerful teeth. Felix felt his heart pounding.

He couldn't help thinking only one thing was missing from this amazing morning: he wished Flo was there to share the scene with him.

CHAPTER 13

MONKEYING AROUND

The rest of the morning was just as wonderful, although they did not see any more big cats. Felix was secretly hoping to see a leopard, as he knew from his *Big Book of Safari Facts* that this was the hardest cat to find.

'They sleep in the trees and even drag their prey up there to eat because they are Completely Camouflaged under the foliage and light that filters through the leaves,' he told Zed earnestly.

They saw so many other wonderful things, though, that it didn't matter about not seeing a leopard. At one point they came across a clearing where a family of banded mongoose, just like Kabelo, were digging in giant pinky-red termite mounds, squabbling with each other and chasing and nipping at each other's tails.

'How did you get hold of Kabelo to give him to Mo?' Felix asked Bibi at one point. 'They move so fast!'

Bibi chuckled. 'I hope you are not thinking of trying to catch a pet for yourself,' he said.

Felix flushed a deep red, and dipped his face so that the visor on his baseball cap hid his cheeks. 'It's just that I can't see how you could have done it.'

'I did not catch him exactly,' said Bibi. 'I found him when he was very sick. He could have died if I had not taken him to the sanctuary where they care for the animals that are ill.'

'You take wild animals to a vet?' asked Mum in disbelief.

'Sometimes we have to – there are specially trained vets who have to come into the reserve occasionally to help sick animals. Usually it is not for a creature like a mongoose, as the mongoose is not a protected animal. We do have to let nature take its course. But I love animals so much, if I see a sick animal and I can safely help it, I will always try,' said Bibi. He chuckled. 'I made my father so cross when I was young! He was a hunter and he did not see the point of helping animals to get better. I was always bringing creatures home and hiding them in the village and in our hut. My father would say,

"One day you will be a man and you will not be able to do this any more. You will be a hunter like me." But then I studied and passed my exams to work in conservation, and that is how I became a game driver. I never wanted to grow up to kill things like my father.'

Felix was amazed at this story. 'So you *saved* Kabelo?'

Bibi nodded. 'Yes. But the problem was that he got used to humans. Now he will not go back to the wild. So really, I think it was not a very sensible thing to do.'

'Did you hear that, Felix?' Mum said, glaring at him. 'So don't go getting any ideas!'

'Yeah, but it was kind, man,' said Zed admiringly.

'Yes,' said Felix. 'It was.'

They stayed watching the mongoose family for a while longer. Felix thought it was funny how much like human children they were. He imagined Sophie Disbry and Millie Hampton as the two cross, bossy mongoose, jabbering at the smaller ones. Then a bigger, even bossier one came along and split up the group. That's Flo, Felix said to himself.

'Time to head back for a proper second breakfast!' Bibi announced.

'Already?' Felix was sure they had only just started out on their drive.

'Too right, man!' said Zed, making a big show of rubbing his tummy. 'I'm starving. It's nearly eleven o'clock.'

Bibi turned the jeep around and they headed back to the camp. They passed a herd of zebra grazing. While Felix was filming them, some giraffes lolloped by, their ridiculously long necks waving like bulrushes.

'Did you know that a giraffe's neck has

only seven bones in it?' Felix said. 'And that is really weird because humans only have seven too!'

'That can't be right,' said Mum.

'It is, *Mma*,' said Bibi. 'Their necks are very muscly. They use them to fight, you know, as well as to reach the leaves at the top of trees!'

'Wow, I would love to see them fight!' said Felix.

'Fighting's not cool, man,' said Zed gravely.

Bibi laughed. 'You were the one asking me about nature taking its course!' he teased. 'I would like to see you tell a lion not to hunt or a cheetah not to kill. They have to do this to live.'

Zed nodded. 'I know. But it's kinda sad.'

'Not really,' said Bibi. 'It is survival. What is sad is when man comes and kills for sport. My father used to hunt the big game: lion, rhino and so on, to sell. That was sad. Man never kills big game to eat. But animals kill other animals because they have to in order to survive. Even in conservation we have to understand about the food chain.'

Felix drank in every word.

He was about to ask some more questions when there was a loud cackling and shrieking from the bush and Bibi had to stop as a horde of monkeys came careering out in front of the jeep.

'Oh no!' Mum cried, covering her head with her hands. 'Not this again!'

Zed reached over the back of his seat and put his hand on Mum. 'Don't worry, sis. Bibi knows what to do. This isn't Shortfleet Safari Park.'

Sure enough, as Bibi revved the engine and began inching towards the group of monkeys, they scattered to the side of the track.

'Remember, they see the jeep as a bigger animal,' Bibi explained. 'They do not see us inside. If I rev the engine, they think we are growling at them, threatening them.'

'Cool!' said Felix. 'But how come they have not completely run away?'

The monkeys were simply sitting on the edge of the track now. Some of them were staring at the

jeep; others were baring their teeth and making
jabbering noises.

'They are curious animals,' said Bibi. 'They like
to show off a bit too. You see those ones making
faces at us? They are trying to prove that they are
brave and strong. It is a warning to us not to mess
with them. But as soon as I do this –' he revved the

engine again – 'they will move back.'

They did! The smaller monkeys shrieked and ran up the nearest tree, and a mother with a baby on her back followed them. The larger males backed off, but did their best to stand their ground at a short distance, puffing out their chests and gnashing their teeth.

Zed chuckled. 'They are just like us, really,' he said.

Mum peered from over the top of Zed's seat. 'Oh, yes?' she said. 'How d'you work that out?'

'Look at the mother up in the tree,' Zed said. 'She's telling her kids off, making sure they are safe and that they don't run into danger.'

As he said this, the mother grabbed a particularly bouncy young male and gave him a slap! Then she tweaked his ear and sent him packing with a screech.

Everyone laughed.

'At least I never do that!' said Mum.

'Look at that one, sitting on the branch above the mother!' said Felix.

The monkey had been surreptitiously picking nuts out of the tree and was now hurling them down on the mother. She immediately swung up to him and gave him a cuff around the ears too!

Felix captured the entire scene on film.

If I watch them closely enough, he thought, I might come up with a plan of how to get one to take home for Flo. I wish Mo was here right now. I bet she would help me.

He looked at the adults. There was no way he was going to be able to get his hands on a monkey with them around.

CHAPTER 14

FELIX SHARES HIS SECRET

They arrived back at camp to find Elvis and Mo had cooked a huge 'second breakfast' of scrambled eggs, bacon, beans and sausages, with more tea and more toast.

'Sweet!' cried Zed, rubbing his stomach. 'A Full English in the middle of the African bush!'

Everyone ate far too much, and then the adults ambled off into the shade to snooze as the sun was high

in the sky by now and the temperature had risen considerably.

'I do wish I could find my sunglasses and hat,' Mum mumbled. She was so drowsy, however, following her early morning wake-up call, and with the food and the heat, that she was soon fast asleep on a lounger in the shade.

Felix didn't want to sleep. Mum had told him to go into the tent, but his head was buzzing with everything he had seen that morning; his ears were ringing with the sounds of the bush, the birds and creatures calling out to one another in alarm or to attract each other; his skin felt warm from the growing heat as the sun rose to its highest point.

He waited until he was sure the adults were asleep: Bibi was flat on his back in his hammock, snoring softly, Zed was next to Mum on a lounger under the mess canopy, and Elvis was in another hammock, dozing while listening to his iPod.

Felix beckoned to Mo to come close so that he

could be sure no one would wake up and overhear or interrupt. He took a deep breath and plunged straight in.

'Mo, I need your help,' he said.

'OK, OK, why are you whispering?' Mo asked.

Felix moved closer to Mo. 'I don't want anyone else to hear.'

'Oh, a secret! Good!' said Mo, grabbing him by the arm and dragging him away from the sleeping adults.

'So, what is this secret?' Mo asked, once they were safely out of earshot.

'It's about a friend of mine,' he said.

'A girl friend or a boy friend?' Mo asked.

Felix hesitated. 'Well, she's a girl . . .' he began.

'Hold it!' said Mo, her hand in the air. 'I thought you told me that you did not want to be anyone's boyfriend, hmmm?'

Felix stammered, 'I – I – no, I don't.'

'And now you are telling me that you have a *Girl Friend*?' Mo persisted.

Felix shook his head, 'No, no, no! Listen! That is not the point. I have a friend who is a girl and she is called Flo . . .'

Mo burst into fits of giggles and pushed Felix lightly away. 'Aww, that is charming!' she said. 'Why did you just not say that you wanted me to be your girlfriend?'

Felix looked horrified. 'NO! I said "*Flo*", not "Mo"! I mean – I didn't mean to offend you,' he said hastily, as he watched Mo's expression darken into a scowl. 'Please, Mo, will you just listen to everything first before you say something else?' he pleaded.

Mo shrugged and sat back with her arms folded. 'OK,' she yawned. 'But hurry up, because I am getting bored of this secret.'

Felix stuck out his bottom lip. Why were girls such hard work? Maybe this was why his older brother Merv was always in such a bad mood? Maybe girls just got harder and harder work so that by the time you were Merv's age they drove you potty.

'So, I have this friend called Flo – Flora,' he

corrected himself quickly, 'and she is a girl, but she is *not* my girlfriend. And she loves animals as much as I do.'

'So? I am a girl and I love animals,' Mo muttered.

Felix chose to ignore her and went on, 'And Flo-*ra* –' he cleared his throat – 'Flora has asked me to bring her back something from Africa,' he said. 'Only she has asked me for something quite difficult and I don't know if I can manage it.'

'Oh, so you want me to *help* you do this so that you can show off to your friend-who-is-a-girl when you get back to England?' Mo said. Her dark eyes had a steely glint to them, Felix couldn't help noticing.

'Y-yes.' He faltered. 'Cos the thing is –' he let out a heavy sigh – 'she is going to make life rather difficult for me back home if I don't.'

Felix hated himself for admitting this. Mo was bound to think he was weak and a bit of a weirdo now.

However, Mo perked up suddenly. 'If I help you, will you give me an excellent present which you have brought me from England?' she said. She had her hands on her hips and was smiling at him in what he thought looked quite a dangerous and challenging sort of way.

'I – er. Oh . . .' said Felix. What on earth was he supposed to say to that? 'I didn't bring any presents. I – I didn't actually know that I was going to meet you,' he pointed out.

'Well, you should have found out from Mr Zed,' said Mo. Her smile was fading fast. 'You knew you were meeting my daddy. Why did you not know you were meeting me? All I can say is, if you do not get a present for me, why should I help you to get a present for your English Girl Friend?'

Felix felt all the air go out of him as though he was a balloon that someone had stuck a pin into. Mo did have a point, he realized.

'You can have my head torch if you like?' he
offered. He did not really want to give his head torch
away, but he couldn't think of anything else.

'Pfff,' Mo said. 'I do not need a torch. I can see in
the dark.'

Felix was pretty sure this was not true, but Mo
was looking so disdainful he decided it was not
worth arguing with her. He felt that the opportunity
of getting Mo on his side was slipping away fast, so
he said, 'What sort of a present *would* you like? If
you gave me a clue, I could see what I could find.'

'Ha! I am not going to make things that easy for
you, Felix,' Mo scoffed. 'But,' she added slyly, 'when
you have found something nice for *me*, I will ask
my daddy about finding something special for your
"friend". OK?'

'OK,' Felix said. He had no idea how he would
manage this, but he was desperate to get the
conversation back on track. 'Only,' he went on,
'the thing I need – well, I was kind of hoping that

we could keep this a secret between us two, you know – not let the boring grown-ups know?'

Mo struggled to maintain a bored expression, but Felix could see she was intrigued. Eventually she said, 'All right.'

Felix swallowed. Then he said, 'I need you to help me get a monkey – a baby monkey.'

Mo stared at him in silence for a moment. Then she leaned in and shouted, 'A WHAT?' and let out a volley of hyena-laughs, throwing her head back and showing all her white teeth.

'Shhhh!' said Felix, looking around wildly. 'You'll wake the others!'

Mo shook her head at him. 'You want me to trap a baby monkey – this is the present you want to give your Girl Friend in England?'

Felix nodded miserably. 'I know. It's hopeless, isn't it?'

Mo shrugged. 'It is not so hopeless, no,' she said carelessly.

'Not for someone like me. But you will have to give me a ve-ry spe-ci-al present in return,' she drawled.

'OK, OK!' cried Felix. 'Anything!'

'Anything?'

Felix gulped and nodded. 'Uh-huh.'

A cunning smile crept slowly from the corners of Mo's mouth until it lit up her entire face. 'Fine. In that case . . . I would like your camera.'

Felix felt his stomach plummet into his sandals. 'My what?' he whispered. 'I can't do that. It's not mine: it's my dad's.'

'OK.' Mo shrugged again. 'No camera, no monkey,' she said.

She stuck her nose in the air and turned around, leaving Felix feeling powerless to respond.

CHAPTER 15

THE TREE OF LIFE

Felix did not enjoy the late afternoon game drive as much as the morning. He was too preoccupied. He sat hunched against his uncle, staring vacantly at the passing landscape as Bibi gave a running commentary on the birdlife around them. 'And that is a hamerkop – it means "hammer-head". Can you see that its head is shaped like a hammer? And that small bird with the blue and lilac colouring – that is the lilac-breasted roller. It is our national bird,' Bibi said with pride.

Felix sighed.

'Feels, man . . .' Zed shook him gently. 'Are you falling asleep? You are a bit dopey this evening. And you keep, like, sighing – you're not sick, are you?'

'I told you to have a sleep in the afternoon,' said Mum.

'No, I'm not tired,' said Felix. 'I'm not sick either.'

Zed frowned. 'Well, you're not yourself. Did you have a fight with Mo?'

Felix chewed the inside of his cheek. He did not want to get Mo into trouble, because he still needed her help. 'No,' he said. How *was* he going to get Mo to help him, though? No way could he give her Dad's camera. He would be in so much trouble if anything happened to—

'Oh!' he cried, sitting bold upright. 'The camera!'

'What have you done with it?' Mum said with a gasp. 'You'd better not have lost it—'

'No, I've left it behind,' Felix said, slumping back against Zed.

'Well, I'm not sure that was a safe thing to do,' said Mum.

'Chill, sis,' said Zed.

'It will be OK, *Mma*,' said Bibi. 'Mo and Elvis are there. It will be perfectly safe, as long as you closed the tent.'

'You did close the tent, didn't you?' Mum asked.

'Sis, it's cool. I closed it,' Zed assured her. 'Hey, Bibi, how about we show Feels the Tree of Life?'

Bibi turned and grinned. 'An excellent idea,' he said. 'I know just the place.'

'What is the Tree of Life?' Felix asked.

'The baobab, man,' said Zed. 'It's the coolest tree in the world. A spot of real African magic.'

Bibi tutted. 'Zed, it is not magic. It is true there are many myths and legends about the baobab, but . . . why don't you see for yourself?'

They pulled up by the strangest tree Felix had ever seen.

Mum laughed. 'It looks as though it has been planted upside down!' she said.

'There is an old story,' said Bibi. 'They used to say that an elephant frightened the ancestor of the baobab, which is why it grows upside down – it buried its head in the earth to escape the elephant.'

The tree had strange, thin wiry branches which looked more like roots, whereas its roots were thick and heavy, crawling along the surface of the ground for quite a way before burrowing down into the dark red, dusty soil.

Felix got out of the jeep and went over to the tree with Bibi.

'The bark . . . it's freaky,' said Felix. He reached out and touched it. 'It's like skin!'

The bark was a pinky-brown.

'I think the trunk actually looks like an elephant's leg,' said Mum. 'Are you sure this is a tree? Maybe the elephant in the story got frightened instead and buried itself in the ground?'

Bibi laughed. 'I do not think you like the look of my Tree of Life? Ah, but you will be amazed at what it can do.'

He took a penknife from the jeep and went over to the tree. Then he crouched down next to one of the big roots and began to gouge a hole in the bark. He made a hole as big as his fist.

'Come,' he said to Felix, nodding and waving to him.

Felix looked at Zed, who grinned encouragingly, then he went over to Bibi.

'Put your hand in here,' he said, pointing to the hole.

'Bibi, it is safe, isn't it?' asked Mum. 'I mean, there won't be any snakes or anything like that in there?'

Bibi shook his head. 'Watch,' he said. He put his own hand in the hole and brought it out. No snakes or spiders came out with it – only water! A fistful of water, which Bibi tipped into his mouth and drank, making a big show of how delicious it was, smacking his lips and laughing.

'Wow!' said Felix. He plunged his hand in too. 'There's a whole lake of water in there!' he cried, as he brought his hand out, dripping wet.

'See? African magic,' said Zed, winking.

'Well, it is true that there are many stories about the powers of the baobab tree,' said Bibi, stroking the roots. 'Long ago, people did think that it really *was* magic that you could get water from the tree. Also it has medicinal properties, so you could say that is magic too. For example, the leaves are rich in vitamin C and calcium. Perhaps this is why many people have believed that a man who takes a drink made from the bark will become strong. And in some places people still think that a baby boy should be bathed in such a liquid, as this will make him grow into a strong man.'

Felix listened carefully. 'So, you mean that the tree is like a vegetable which is good for humans? Like when Mum says I should eat my greens and that will make me strong? I've never believed that. I thought she was just saying it to make me eat them.'

Bibi grinned. 'Your mother is a wise woman,' he said.

'Thank you,' said Mum, smiling. 'At last my talents are recognized.'

'Sometimes we eat the leaves of the baobab because of the good vitamins,' Bibi continued. 'They can be cooked, you see, like cabbage.'

Felix pulled a face.

'Cabbage is good!' said Bibi. 'The root of a very young baobab tree is delicious, too!'

Felix shook his head, 'Yeuch!' he cried. Why did

grown-ups describe vegetables as 'delicious'? Did something happen to your taste buds when you grew up? Or did grown-ups just say those things to try and trick children?

Bibi went on, 'The seeds are good to eat too. And when the wood is chewed, it can quench your thirst. There are other things people have said for hundreds and thousands of years about the tree. Some tribes worship the baobab as a symbol of fertility. Again, there is truth in this, I think – the goodness of the bark and the leaves, and the wonderful way it keeps water for us, make it a very fertile plant. Many people plant a new baobab from seeds they have kept when they move village.

So we know it is special.'

Felix wished he could take some African magic home for Flo. It would be easier than secretly catching a baby monkey, that was for sure.

CHAPTER 16

A NASTY SHOCK

Felix was feeling unhappier by the minute. He still had not thought of a better present for Mo and he knew he could not give her the camera.

He watched Elvis scrape out the frying pan and chuck the remnants on to the camp fire where they sizzled.

I feel like those scrapy bits, thought Felix. He sighed and shuffled over to the mess where Mo was laying the table.

He tried talking to her about the baobab tree and the other things he had seen that afternoon.

Mo would not look at him. She only said, 'Have you thought about giving me the camera?' and when

141

Felix said no, she turned away, saying, 'No camera, no monkey.'

Luckily Zed was on hand to make Felix feel less glum. His uncle was always good at this. He seemed to have a sixth sense when it came to what was on Felix's mind.

'Hey, dude,' he said, coming over. 'Some more elephants have come into the camp. They've eaten way too much marula, man! It's hilarious! Why don't you get the camera and film them to make up for missing out this afternoon?'

Sure enough, the elephants were weaving clumsily in and out of the trees, their trunks waving about uncontrollably, their feet unsteady. They did look funny, and the sight cheered Felix up. He and Zed laughed together at the sight of the big lumbering elephants, falling over their own feet, woozy with the fermented fruit they loved so much.

'Flo would love this, wouldn't she?' said Zed. 'Hey, dude, why don't you put a film together just for her of all the funny things that animals do? She's always looking at those clips on the Internet of kittens falling over and dogs wearing hats and stuff.'

Felix was not sure. 'Maybe,' he said.

Zed nudged him. 'Bet she's never seen a clip of an elephant behaving like this!'

Felix gave a small smile. 'OK, I'll get the camera.'

Zed grinned. 'Sweet, man! You'd better hurry up in case they move on.'

Felix went round to the front of his tent. He stopped in the doorway. Something did not look right.

It was his rucksack. The bag was open and Felix's *Big Book of Safari Facts* had been dumped carelessly upside down on the bed so that the spine was cracked. Other stuff was spilling out on to his sleeping bag, too: his torch, a pack of cards, some boiled sweets and a packet of tissues.

That's odd, he thought. I'm sure I put the bag under the camp bed. And I know I zipped it up. I certainly didn't leave all my stuff falling out like that.

He went to pick up the book and smoothed its rumpled pages. That was when he realized what was really bothering him.

'The camera –! OH NO!' His hands flew to his mouth.

The camera had gone!

Felix's first instinct was to run out of the tent and shout his discovery to the whole camp, but then his throat seized up with fear, as he knew Mum would go Totally Ballistic when he told her he had lost Dad's camera.

Then he remembered Mo, turning away from him, her nose in the air: 'No camera, no monkey.'

Surely she wouldn't steal the camera? Felix felt a bit sick.

'Zed will help,' he said to himself. 'I will have to tell Zed, and get him to swear that he will help me to look for it without anyone else knowing.'

Zed would not freak out and shout at him, as Mum most certainly would. And he would not start to rant and rave about how Money Does Not Grow On Trees and how Felix would have to save all of his pocket money From Here Until Kingdom Come so that he could pay for a new one. And he would not rush in and accuse Mo and shout and complain to Bibi. No. Zed would keep calm and know what to do.

Even as Felix told himself this, he was not really convinced. It actually did look as though someone had gone through his stuff to take the camera, after all; not that he had simply mislaid it.

There was nothing for it: Felix had to tell someone, and Zed was undoubtedly the best person to tell.

So he walked out of the tent, forcing his face into what he hoped was a natural-looking smile.

Unfortunately Mum was right outside the tent.

'What's the matter with you? You look as though you're in pain,' she said. 'You *have* got a tummy bug, haven't you? You've been acting strangely all day. Oh no, I hope you aren't sickening for something. What will we do . . . ?'

'Er, sis,' Zed stepped in between Mum and Felix. 'I think he's just, like, smiling?'

Felix nodded. 'I am just soooo happy!' he said,

with a slight wobble in his voice.

Zed peered at him closely. 'Hey, Feels! Why don't we go for a little walk.'

Mum shook her head. 'I don't think that's a good idea. It might not be safe. If Felix is not feeling well – hang on a minute . . . I thought Zed said you were about to film those elephants?'

Felix felt his chest go icy cold. 'N-no,' he said, shaking his head emphatically. 'I went to get some, er, sweets to share with Mo. But I couldn't find any. Must have finished them. I would like to go for a walk with Zed, actually. He'll look after me, don't worry. You carry on reading your book, Mum. You're always saying you never have enough Me Time,' he added for good measure.

Mum narrowed her eyes in suspicion at this unusual show of concern for her wellbeing. Then she shrugged and said, 'OK,' and did as Felix suggested.

Once she was out of range, Zed put a long lanky arm around his nephew and leaned down to whisper, 'Phew, thought she'd never leave!'

Felix puffed out his cheeks and breathed, 'Yes.'

'So, come on. What's up, little dude?'

Felix looked up at his uncle. The corners of his mouth wobbled. 'I've lost it!' he said, in a panicky whisper. 'Dad's camera – it's gone!'

'Oh, man!' Zed gasped. 'Are you sure? How? When?'

Felix shook his head. 'I don't know. I thought it was in my bag under my bed. But just now I looked and everything was spilt on to the sleeping bag, and the camera wasn't there!'

Zed stroked his beard thoughtfully. The beads in it clicked gently. Then he scratched his head and began pacing to and fro. 'I'll start by asking Bibi who's been in the camp today,' he said.

'Oh no, don't do that,' Felix pleaded. 'I don't want anyone else to know . . .' He hesitated and wondered if he should mention the conversation with Mo. But then he would have to tell about the monkey too, and he did not think that was a good idea, even with Zed. What if his uncle said something to Mum?

'Please!' he pleaded. 'Can you help me look?'

Zed looked at Felix sadly. 'Dude, it doesn't sound like you just lost it, does it? Come to think of it, your mum still hasn't found her sunglasses or hat. And this morning I couldn't find any pants.'

Felix started. 'What?' he said.

Zed blushed. 'Yeah, well, I'm not totally tidy all the time, so I didn't think much of it. But, y'know, it's weird these things going missing . . . and a camera? Well, that's serious.'

Felix sighed and swallowed hard. His eyes were starting to sting. He shook his head furiously.

Zed put a large hand on his shoulder and said, 'Listen, let's have a look around first. Then let me talk to Bibi. Trust me, OK?'

Felix reluctantly agreed.

They began by taking a good look under the tent flaps and in the long grass.

'Maybe you just dropped it in the dark earlier in the day?' Zed said. But Felix could tell his uncle was only trying to make him feel less anxious.

They checked on Mum quickly as they passed her,
but she was still engrossed in her book.

'If she asks us what we're doing,' Zed whispered,
'just say you are looking for bugs. She won't want to
come and join us, that's for sure!'

Felix gave a half-hearted laugh. 'No, but she'll

panic and tell us not to, in case the bugs are poisonous,' he muttered.

Suddenly Zed straightened up and waved something he had found at Felix. He called in a stage whisper, 'Look!'

Felix ran lightly towards him, shooting nervous glances in Mum's direction. 'What is it?' he whispered back.

'Lens cap, man!' said Zed. 'Looks like someone dropped it. Let's go over to the kitchen area next, see if we can pick up any more clues.'

'B-but . . . Bibi and the others will be there,' Felix said.

Zed tapped a long finger against the side of his nose. 'It's cool. I'll distract him while you take a look.'

They searched behind the jeep. Felix caught sight of a black shape. He bent down and fished it out.

'The case!' he hissed.

Zed looked horrified. 'Oh, man . . .'

Felix frowned. 'What?'

Zed glanced at Bibi, who looked back and said, 'Dinner will be ready very soon!'

'Sweet!' called Zed, with a nervous grin. Then he gestured to Felix to move away so that they could speak without fear of being heard. 'You don't think . . .' he hesitated. 'I mean, this is really embarrassing, man – you don't seriously think one of these guys would take your camera?'

Felix bit his lip. 'I don't know,' he said. 'It couldn't be Bibi. He has been with us all the time. And Elvis has been busy cooking, so I don't think it's him.'

'Anyway, Feels, we haven't actually found the camera yet,' Zed hastily pointed out. 'Finding the lens cap and the case doesn't prove anything.'

Felix nodded glumly. They went quietly back to the hammock area to continue their search. As Felix approached Mo's hammock, he had a creeping sensation that he was about to discover something that he would not like. What if Mo had decided to take the camera? No, she would not be that mean . . .

And that is when he saw it – in her hammock!
Nestled against a bunched-up mosquito net.

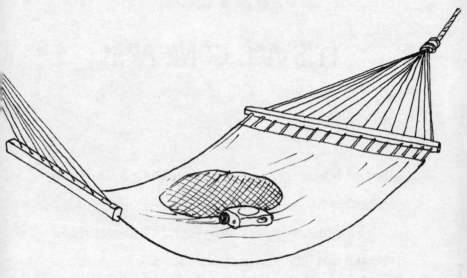

Felix was rooted to the spot, staring at it.

'Oh no . . .' Zed breathed.

Felix swallowed. He was about to ask what
they should do, when a voice said, 'And tell me,
Feeeliix, what do you think you are doing with my
hammock?'

CHAPTER 17

IT'S ALL GONE APE!

Felix and Mo stared at each other for a beat. Then they both started shouting at once.

'Well what are YOU doing with MY camera?'

'I have not TOUCHED your camera!'

'SO WHAT IS IT DOING IN YOUR HAMMOCK?'

'I DON'T KNOW – YOU MUST HAVE PUT IT THERE!'

'Hey! Hey! GUYS!' Zed pleaded, stepping in between Felix and Mo.

Bibi came rushing over. 'What is all this?' he demanded.

Zed raised his eyebrows. 'Bit of a disagreement, man. I'm sure we can sort it peacefully, eh, guys?' He had a hand gently on each child, separating them.

Mo tried to shrug him off and let out a low
growling sound. Felix was trembling.

Zed looked at them in turn. 'You gotta chill. I have
an idea. Why don't we take a look at the film on the
camera and see what's been going on? You won't
mind, will you, Mo?'

'Of course I do not mind, you stupid—'

'HARMONY!' Bibi reprimanded. 'What is this about a camera?' he asked Zed.

'Felix had mislaid his dad's camera. We happened to find it here, but—'

Mo butted in loudly, 'LOOK AT THE FILM! I keep telling you, I did not take it. Felix was probably filming ME!'

'I WAS NOT!'

'You are filming everything, all the time, being a snooping little—'

Zed hastily grabbed the camera from the hammock and turned it on. As the screen flicked into life, everyone stopped talking to crowd around it.

Felix peered closely at the scene unfolding before him, while Zed breathed in sharply and whispered, 'Oh, man . . .'

The footage was of Zed. At first it was quite boring. He was just ambling around outside the tent. Felix thought the film must have been made just before they had left for their game drive that afternoon, as Mum could be seen, just inside the frame, packing the small bag with sun cream and snacks. Felix wondered how Mo could have got hold of the camera at this point. What had *he* been doing, he wondered?

Suddenly Mo let forth a snort of laughter as Zed began laboriously picking his nose. He clearly did not know that anyone was watching him, let alone filming him, because he had a good old rummage in one nostril before extracting his finger to inspect what he had discovered. He then glanced around quickly and popped the results into his mouth.

'Yeeeeuuuckk!' said Mo. 'That is *very* disgusting.'

Bibi jabbed her in the ribs, but Felix was sniggering now as well.

'Hey, man,' said Zed looking hurt, 'I didn't know I was on film, did I – Wow! Oh no, my sis is not going to like this . . .'

The camera had panned around to zoom in on Mum now. She could just be seen in the interior of the tent, struggling out of her shorts, clearly with a view to changing into some longer trousers for the game drive. She obviously did not know anyone could see her. She had got one foot caught in the fabric of the shorts while she was taking them off. Then she lost her balance and toppled backwards, falling flat on her bottom.

Mo let rip with one of her loudest hyena-laughs. Felix chewed on his cheeks to try to stop himself from laughing too. Even if Mo had taken the camera, he felt he might be able to forgive her for making such a funny film.

Then the screen went fuzzy for a second.

158

REC
0.12.08

'Phew, that's it then,' Zed began. 'Could have been worse, I guess . . .'

Then, just as he said this, there was a funny grunting sound and some heavy breathing and the film started up again.

'Oh no! Me and my big mouth!' Zed wailed, burying his head in his hands.

'Is that you in the bathroom, Mr Zed?' Mo gasped.

Felix went bright red: they were watching footage of his uncle in the shower! The person taking the film had somehow been able to get above the cubicle and was aiming the camera down to get a bird's eye view of poor Zed. Luckily his long snaky hair did a lot to hide him, so all Felix could see was a wet and bedraggled mop of long hair.

'You look like a giant yellow baboon caught out in the rain!' Mo sniggered.

'Turn it off!' Zed wailed, peering through his fingers at the image.

'Yes, I agree. I think we have seen enough,' said Bibi.

But before anyone could press the 'off' button, the picture changed to show Felix – on the loo! This was also an aerial view.

Felix whirled round to face Mo. 'How could you be so mean?' he shouted, snatching the camera from Zed.

Mo had been giggling hard but when Felix turned on her, she stopped and looked horrified. 'But – you do not still think it was *me*?' she gasped. She looked to her father and Zed for support, but both adults said nothing. Bibi looked stony-faced, whereas Zed just looked embarrassed. He shifted his gaze away from the little girl and shook his head sadly.

'Harmony, I think you and I had better have a talk,' said Bibi, taking his daughter by the arm and leading her away.

He began talking at speed in Setswana in an even angrier tone than he had used after the spider incident.

'Dude, I am so sorry,' Zed whispered. 'Bibi told me that Harmony had never come on a trip with tourists before, and that he was only letting her if she behaved. He thought it would give her a chance to grow up and prove she could be more mature. I guess that was a fail. And I thought you guys would end up really good mates . . .'

Felix was not listening, however. He had heard another sound coming from the camera. The film was still running. The noises were very strange: they were sort of like laughter, but not like laughter from any person Felix knew. He peered at the screen which was still fuzzy.

'Oooo-waaah-ha-ha-ha-haaaa! Oooo-Oooo! Waaaa-hahahaha!'

Zed heard the noises too. He stopped talking and leaned in to take a look at the fuzzy screen. 'Man, if I didn't know better, I'd say that noise sounds exactly like—'

'Wait! Look at that!' cried Felix. He grabbed Zed's arm and pointed at the screen.

It was Mo. Mo was on film.

'How did she . . . ? She must have set it to auto . . .' Zed muttered.

Mo had been caught on camera sneaking some snacks from the kitchen area. She was stuffing them into her mouth, checking over her shoulder now and then to make sure no one was watching.

'Freaky,' breathed Zed. 'She couldn't have filmed herself, cos she wouldn't want anyone to know she'd been filching stuff . . . which means, she couldn't have been filming us either so . . .'

'. . . someone must have been filming *her*!' Felix exclaimed. 'We must show Bibi. Quick!' Felix made to run over to his friends, but Zed put a hand on his shoulder to stop him.

'Feels, I think we should watch *everything* before we rush in. Maybe she just left the camera running by mistake while she went to get a snack. Maybe we'll see her pick it up in a minute and – holy cow!'

Felix saw Zed's face freeze with shock and followed his uncle's gaze to the screen. The film was still running, but now it was not Mo's face on the screen. It was . . .

'Monkeys?' said Felix in disbelief. 'MONKEYS! Oh my goodness! Bibi, Mo, come and look at this!'

The camera was now evidently being passed from monkey to monkey.

'Boy, are they having fun!' Zed whispered.

'They've got our clothes!' Felix gasped. He waved frantically at Bibi to stop him from talking to Mo. 'Look!' he shouted. 'They're wearing Mum's hat and sunglasses and – oh dear,' he added more quietly as something occurred him. 'Someone must have left the tent open!'

'Oh, man!' Zed cried. Then he checked himself

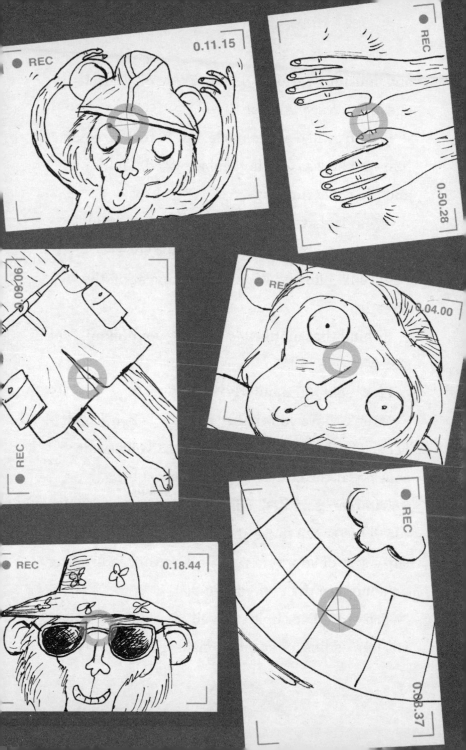

and, blushing furiously, said, 'Er, yeah, yeah. I guess . . . *someone* must have.'

Felix frowned at his uncle, but before he could ask him why he was looking embarrassed, Mum, Bibi and Mo came running.

'What is that racket? Is that Dad's . . . What's going on . . . ?' Mum faltered, as she too saw what Zed, Felix, Bibi and Mo were looking at on the screen.

'I think that monkey is wearing your bikini, *Mma*,' said Mo.

'Yes,' said Mum quietly. 'Very fetching.'

'Aren't those your pants too, Uncle Zed?' said Felix. 'On the little one's head?' His voice went squeaky at the end as he said this last bit.

'Hmmm,' said Zed. His voice was going squeaky too. 'I recognize those shorts too,' he added, letting slip a sort of snorty noise. 'Reckon they look better on a monkey than on you, dude.'

Felix could not hold himself together any longer. His pursed lips burst open, making a raspberry farting sound and suddenly he was laughing and laughing and laughing, so hard he thought that he might actually have stopped breathing. Zed and Mum joined in, clutching at their sides and pointing at the film, gasping, 'Oh my goodness, that is too funny!'

Bibi was smiling and shaking his head, saying, 'Well, I never saw such a thing.'

The only person who was not joining in was Mo.

'I am glad you are all so HAPPY!' she shouted.

Everyone immediately stopped giggling and looked at her. She had her hands on her hips and her face was thunderous.

'W-what's the matter, Mo?' Felix stammered.

'What is the MATTER?' Mo cried. 'I will tell you what the matter is, Feeeliiix. *You* blamed *me* for the missing camera and the film of you on the toilet and your uncle in the shower and your mother getting undressed. And now you see that it was not *me* at all, it was these monkeys, and you think it is FUNNY?'

'Harmony,' Bibi said, reaching out to touch her

shoulder. 'Can you not see that it is amusing?'

Mo pulled away. 'NO!'

'At least everyone now knows it was not your fault,' said Bibi.

'I'm sorry, Mo,' said Felix. 'I should have trusted you.'

'Yes,' said Mum. 'We are sorry.'

Mo crossed her arms tightly across her chest and frowned even harder. 'What about you, Mr Zed?' she said, 'Hmm?'

Zed looked sheepish too. 'Like, sorry, Mo.'

Then Mo shot Felix a strange look: a sort of sparkly-eyed mischievous look. 'All right,' she said. 'I will forgive all of you.'

The atmosphere lifted as Mo smiled at Felix. 'Thanks,' he said.

'Good, that is settled,' said Bibi. 'Let's eat!'

Everyone began making their way over to the table, chattering and laughing about the monkeys. Felix walked with Mo. He smiled at her, feeling relieved that he had been forgiven. He was about to suggest that she borrow his camera as a kind of peace offering.

But then he saw that Mo was no longer smiling at him. Instead she had fixed him with a steely glare.

Felix felt his stomach lurch.

Mo leaned in so that the adults would not hear. Then she hissed into Felix's ear. *'I am not finished with you, Mr Feeeliiix. You had better watch out.'*

CHAPTER 18

MO IS ON A ROLL

The next day, Mo waited until the adults were resting in the heat again. Then she grabbed Felix by the arm and whispered, 'Come with me.'

Felix reluctantly followed as Mo slipped away from the grown-ups and sat in the shade of a tree.

Mo put her head on one side and regarded Felix thoughtfully. She was quiet for a bit too long and Felix began to feel uncomfortable.

'Why are you looking at me like that?' he whispered.

Mo held up a finger for him to be quiet. She checked that no one was nearby, then she beckoned

to Felix to lean in closer so that she could say in a
low voice, 'I have a plan to get you a monkey.'

Felix swallowed. 'You do? I thought you were still
cross with me from yesterday. And anyway, I'm not
sure it's such a good idea. Now that I've seen what
they did—'

'What is the matter with you?' Mo hissed. 'Are you
a chicken or a boy?'

'I – I'm a boy,' said Felix, not liking the tone Mo's
voice had taken.

'Good. Then you will do as I say. Otherwise your

English Girl Friend will call you a chicken too, I think, hmm?'

Felix sighed. He recognized these tactics. Mo was On A Roll.

'I have been thinking about this Girl Friend of yours,' Mo went on. 'She must be pretty special if you are so worried about getting her the right present,' she said.

Felix blushed. 'It's not that,' he mumbled.

'Oh, so is it that you are *frightened* of this girl, then?' Mo said, a triumphant note creeping into her voice. 'You are frightened of monkeys and you are frightened of girls! Ha!'

'NO!' Felix protested.

'Shhh!' Mo put her finger to her lips and nodded towards the grown-ups. 'They will hear us.'

Felix was trapped.

'This is what I understand,' Mo went on. 'Your English Girl Friend has made a bet with you to get her a monkey and you are worried that she will do something to you if you do not succeed?'

 172

Felix shook his head furiously. 'I just wanted to get her what she asked for because I feel bad about her not being here. She loves animals and she has always wanted to come to Africa.'

Mo's face seemed to have softened when Felix mentioned the words 'animals' and 'Africa'.

'Oh, that is very sad,' she said. 'So why could she not come to my country with you? Is she sick?'

Felix almost said, 'Yes,' just to shut her up, but then he was not very good at lying, and he thought if Mo was beginning to feel sorry for Flo, then perhaps she would understand if he just told her the truth.

So he explained about how he and Flo had been making the Natural History Documentary together and how Flo had wanted so much to come to Africa to make a proper film. Then he told Mo about the time Flo had decided to try and steal the monkeys at Shortfleet Safari Park and how it had not worked.

Mo listened carefully. Then she said, 'But tell me, why does your friend want so much to have a monkey as a pet?'

'Well, why do you want to have a mongoose as a pet?' he said.

'That is obvious,' said Mo. 'Kabelo is furry and cuddly and funny.'

'Well, that's what Flo would say about monkeys,' Felix pointed out.

'Hmm,' said Mo.

Felix did not like the look on Mo's face. 'I really, *really* do NOT want to try and steal a monkey from here any more, you know,' he said hastily. 'I have changed my mind now that I have seen how clever they can be. And actually, the monkeys in the park pulled Flo's hair, so if I reminded her of that, she would understand that having a monkey as a pet is not such a good idea . . .'

Mo smiled sweetly. 'That is because they were *captured* monkeys, Felix,' she said. 'They were cross because they were being locked into the park, like you told me. The monkeys here are not like that.'

Felix had a strong suspicion that Mo was not telling the truth.

 174

'But look at what they did with the camera and our clothes and stuff,' said Felix.

'They were being funny and playful!' Mo insisted. 'Anyway, you want only one little baby monkey for your Girl Friend, do you not?'

'I don't understand,' Felix said. 'Why would you want to help me after I nearly got you into so much trouble?'

Mo's eyes flashed. 'I like you, Felix,' she said slyly. Then after a pause, she added. 'Also I need to teach those monkeys a lesson for getting me into trouble.'

CHAPTER 19

FOOD FIGHT!

Mo outlined her plan.

'We are going to set up a little picnic for the monkeys,' she said. 'Nothing tempts a monkey like a table full of food.'

'Won't your dad be cross?' Felix asked.

Mo grinned and raised one eyebrow. 'Only if he finds out.'

Felix was really not sure he wanted to be involved in Mo's plan.

Do all girls go on missions like this? he wondered. Flo was always going on missions. And look where they had got him . . .

Mo, meanwhile, was completely unaware of Felix's

discomfort. She was saying that they should take some food now while the adults were sleeping.

'Come on!' she hissed. 'You must help me. We must do it now – quick!'

Felix unwillingly did as he was told. He followed Mo to the kitchen area and took armfuls of bread rolls and bananas, tomatoes and apples.

'This is the kind of food that the monkeys like,' Mo whispered. 'And *we* do not like all these fruits and vegetables so much, do we? So it will not matter if we take some.'

'Actually, I do like bananas,' Felix muttered.

Mo's behaviour reminded him more and more of Flo. He suddenly remembered the time that Flo had announced that Hammer the hamster should go on holiday, 'because it is unfair to keep him shut up in a cage all the time'. She had convinced Felix that it would be a Very Good Idea to post Hammer in a special box ('that is why it's called Special Delivery, because they treat the box extra-specially carefully') to her cousin who lived by the seaside. Hammer had, thankfully, survived the journey, but Felix had almost not survived when his mum had gone so red in the face he had been convinced that she would explode right there and then, like a bomb or something, and she had made him drive with her all the way to the seaside, which had taken far too many hours, and then made him apologize to Flo's aunt, even though it had not been his fault in the first place.

He had a nasty feeling that he would end up in a similar situation because of Mo's plan, the way things were going.

'OK,' said Mo, as they spread out their haul on the grass. 'I am going to get a cloth and some cutlery and lay the meal out as if I am preparing a proper feast,' she said.

Felix tried to protest that this was a silly idea. Monkeys did not need cutlery.

'But the monkeys will like playing with it, do you not see? It will mean they are so distracted they will not notice when I pounce on one of the babies,' Mo said.

'How will you actually get hold of a baby?' asked Felix. He was feeling a bit sick at the thought of this now – what if a mother monkey got angry with Mo and tried to attack her?

Mo would not be moved, however. She arched one eyebrow. 'I will tell you that in a minute,' she said. 'First, let's put the cutlery out.'

Soon everything was gathered, ready for a feast: the middle of the cloth was piled high with plates of bananas, bowls of tomatoes and apples, and a large basket of bread rolls. Mo had also thoughtfully laid on some drinks for the monkeys in the form of cans of Coke and fizzy orange.

She stood back to survey their handiwork.

'My, that is a picnic fit for a chief,' she said, nodding in a satisfied way. Then she turned to Felix. 'And now you must do as I say. You must climb the tree and take this with you.' She pulled her mosquito net out of her pocket and handed it to him. 'When you see the monkey you want, drop this on it and I will dash out from behind that bush and grab the monkey.'

Felix shuffled his feet in the dust. He desperately tried to think of a way to stop this plan from happening altogether. 'I think I should put the cans of drink away,' he said in a panicky tone. 'That kind of thing is bad for animals.'

Mo rolled her eyes. 'Oh, do not be such a fusspot!' she exclaimed. 'Anyway, if my daddy wakes up now and comes to see what we are doing, he will only think that we are having a little picnic, just the two of us.'

'Hmmm. S'pose,' said Felix. He eyed the mountains of food and drink and thought that there was no way Bibi would fall for that. 'What if the monkeys don't come, after all?' he went on, secretly hoping very much that this would be the case.

Mo sucked her teeth. 'Tcho! They will come. Now, take the net and climb!'

Then she went and sat behind a nearby bush and waited.

Felix stuffed the net into the pocket of his shorts, climbed the tree as far as the lowest branches, and waited. At least it was cool in the shade of the leaves, he thought miserably.

Suddenly there was a thud from another tree somewhere nearby, and a slipping noise, then a chatter and two small vervet monkeys came into view.

Mo peered up at Felix from her hiding place and grinned. 'There!' she rasped. 'I told you they would come.'

The monkeys raced over to the picnic and began grabbing at the bread and bananas.

'There wasn't much point in laying the cutlery out,' Felix muttered to himself.

One of the monkeys had picked up a can of Coke and had managed to hook a finger around the ring-pull and began tugging at it.

Maybe we didn't leave the tent open after all? Felix thought. It certainly looked as though the monkey's nimble fingers were capable of getting inside anything they wanted. In spite of his fears, Felix could not help being amazed as he watched how the monkeys made quick work of the picnic.

The monkey with the can was getting cross. It let out an ear-splitting shriek of fury as it pulled and pulled at the ring on the can, while only a trickle of liquid came out. Then the monkey shook the can ferociously.

Another monkey, who was eating two bananas at once, and had also picked up a bread roll in one of its feet, came over to see what the problem was, snatched the can from its companion and pulled hard at the metal ring. The Coke immediately exploded in a fountain of dark brown, creamy froth, causing both monkeys to screech even louder in surprise.

Felix was terrified the noise would wake Bibi and the others, but Mo simply raised her finger to her lips and shook her head. He reasoned that there was nothing unusual about a monkey shrieking in the bush, so probably no one would come to see what the noise was about.

And he might have been right, were it not for what happened next.

The monkey holding the can of Coke was clearly very angry at being covered in sticky, frothy fizzy drink, and decided to show exactly how annoyed he was by raising the can above his head and hurling it at the first monkey.

The can landed on his companion's head which sent him into a fury as well. He whirled around, grabbed a tomato in each hand and lobbed them at the other monkey's face.

'Mo!' Felix called out, not caring now about waking the others. 'I think we should leave. There are no babies and I'm a bit scared . . .'

But Mo had come out from her hiding place and

was clutching her sides and laughing so hard that tears were pouring down her face. Felix was about to exclaim that there was nothing to laugh about, when there was a colossal thud from above his head and more slipping and sliding sounds, followed by another thud . . . and another and another.

'OH NO!' Felix cried.

Monkey after monkey after monkey raced past him, causing his branch to judder dangerously. They charged at the food and joined in the fray, screeching and jabbering.

Soon there was a seething mass of monkeys on the picnic, picking up cans of Coke and fizzy orange, shaking them and opening them all over one another, picking up bread rolls and tomatoes and chucking them at each other too. (The bananas were clearly seen to be too precious to be used as ammunition – some monkeys who had not joined in the fight were making off with as many of them as they could carry.) It was now impossible to throw the net over an individual monkey, even if Felix had still wanted to. Which he very much did not.

Of course, the noise was so horrendous by this point that Bibi and Elvis had come running. They shouted at the monkeys and waved their arms at them, shooing them away.

That is the moment when one of the monkeys saw Mo, who was still in fits of giggles, and seemed to decide to make a beeline straight for her.

It jumped on to her back and pulled at her hair, then it pounded her with its little fists, screeching all the while, as if to say, 'This is all your fault!'

Poor Mo was screeching too now, and crying, 'Get it off me, get it off!'

Bibi launched himself at the monkey, gripping it by the scruff of its neck. The monkey immediately let go of Mo and began thrashing around to try and free itself. Bibi ran from Mo and threw the monkey into the bush, where it landed, looking dazed for a second. Then it was off, chasing its companions into the trees. The monkeys lobbed the remaining tomatoes and bread rolls at the stunned humans

186

as they ran, gibbering and screaming monkey-insults.

Felix hurtled down the tree and came running to see if Mo was all right. Unfortunately for him, at that exact moment Mum and Zed appeared at his elbow.

'Oh, dude, what have you done?' Zed wailed.

'Felix! Get inside the tent, this minute!' Mum growled.

Mo was sobbing as she rubbed her sore head. 'It's not his fault,' she whimpered.

Bibi looked very upset. He clearly did not know whether to shout at his daughter or to console her. Instead he said, 'Well, whose fault is it?'

Felix stared at the ground. 'I – I'm sorry,' he whispered.

Then he turned and ran to hide in the tent, leaving the adults shaking their heads in bewilderment.

Peace was restored now the monkeys had gone. Only the Grey Louries could be heard above the gentle click-click-whirr of the crickets in the background.

'Go-away! Go-away!' called the birds.

Mum let out the breath she had been holding. 'Do you know, I think we might just do that,' she said. 'I think this camp has had enough of my family for a while.'

188

CHAPTER 20

NO MORE MONKEY MADNESS

Mo and Felix were instructed to clear up the awful mess the monkeys had made. Once Bibi was sure that Mo was suffering from nothing but a few scrapes and bruises, he said he would not listen to any explanations until 'every single piece of food and every can and wrapper is cleared away'.

The children worked in silence; Mo seething and muttering at the unfairness of it all ('After all, am I a monkey? Did I make this mess? No, I did not!'), and Felix feeling utterly ashamed that he had made Bibi, Mum and Zed so cross with him.

This is actually all *Flo's* fault, he thought as he picked up mushed bananas and squashed tomatoes.

189

I don't want to give her a cool present now. In fact, I'm not sure I even care if she's my friend any more.

He felt a rush of heat to his face and battled to keep the tears at bay.

Zed came up behind him. 'Hey, little dude,' he said softly.

'Don't worry. We all know it was Mo's idea.

Even your mum knows you would not have done this without some encouragement.'

Felix looked up at his uncle. His bottom lip began to wobble.

'Feels, don't!' said Zed. He put his arm around him. 'Listen, why don't you tell me what's going on?'

'No, I've got to finish doing this . . .' Felix began. A big, fat tear landed on the front of his T-shirt and spread, leaving a dark splodge.

'It's OK,' Zed said. Then he called out, 'Hey, Feels is just taking a little break. Be back in a jiffy.' Then he quickly marched Felix away from the scattered picnic food before Mo could intervene.

'So,' said Zed. 'Hit me with it.'

'It's all Flo's fault,' Felix began, and let out a shuddery sigh.

Zed frowned. 'Don't you mean Mo?' he said.

Felix shook his head. 'Flo. Flora,' he added, to make it clear who he was talking about. 'She got all huffy with me – I told you.'

'Ye-eah,' said Zed slowly. 'You said you were going to get her a present. It's OK. We've still got time for that. Bibi can stop on the way back and . . . OH!' said Zed. He stopped abruptly. Then he whispered, 'Oh, man – you weren't trying to steal her a monkey?'

Felix nodded glumly.

'MAN!' Zed cried. 'Don't you ever learn your lesson? I thought you'd promised "no more monkey business" after . . .' He broke off as Felix's shoulders began to shake. 'OK, OK. I guess now is not the time. So, what are you going to do?'

Felix sniffed and shrugged. 'I don't know. Flo is going to hate me. She said if I didn't bring her back a monkey there would be No More Us.'

Zed stroked his beard. 'Doesn't sound like she is being much of a friend if she's asking you to do such a stupid thing,' he said.

'You don't understaaaand!' Felix cried.

'OK,' said Zed firmly. 'This is what we are going to do. We're going to explain everything to Bibi and he will come up with a cool idea for something you can take back to Flo which will guarantee that she will be amazed and will still be your friend. How does that sound?'

So Zed took a reluctant Felix to talk to Bibi.

'Bibi, I've been thinking, man,' said Zed. 'Is there, like, anything as cool as the baobab tree, but smaller, obviously, that Felix could take back to impress his friends? He really wants to show them

192

something amazing from your country.'

Bibi raised his eyebrows. 'No animals are allowed to leave the country without a very special licence,' he said.

Zed waved his hand hastily. 'No, no, no! I didn't mean that. Felix has totally learned his lesson about that, haven't you, dude?'

Felix nodded.

Bibi thought for a moment, then he said, 'What about some *tambotie* seeds?'

Zed beamed. 'Yeah, that's the kind of thing.'

'W-what are they?' Felix whispered.

Zed ruffled his hair. 'They're awesome! You could tell Flo they were a little bit of African magic.'

Bibi rolled his eyes. 'I have told you already, there is no such thing. I will get Harmony to show you some *tambotie* seeds and I will explain.' He called over to his daughter who was making a big deal out of picking up the last bits of food from the monkey disaster, and told her to go and find some seeds.

She came back with a handful of things which

looked a bit like tiny snail shells. She also had a cup of water. Then she said to Felix, 'Pour some of this water on your hands.'

Felix looked at Bibi and Zed. They both nodded their encouragement, so he did as she asked. Then he held out his wet hands, palms facing upward and Mo tipped the seeds on to them.

'Oh!' He started, as the seeds immediately began jumping the minute they hit his wet skin. 'What's going on?'

Mo grinned. 'African magic,' she said.

Bibi groaned. 'Stop it, Harmony,' he said. 'Felix, these seeds have small larvae in them – a moth lays its eggs inside the seed. When the rains fall, or any water touches them, the larvae begin to move because they think it is time to hatch, and the seed is dispersed so that new *tambotie* can grow. African children play with these seeds all the time. We call them jumping beans.'

Felix was impressed. However, something told him this was not special enough to impress Flo. 'They are cool,' he said, 'but . . . we have jumping beans at home. Plastic ones,' he admitted, 'but still . . .'

Mo looked cross and was about to protest.

Bibi said hastily, 'Well, I think I can come up with something that you will never have seen before. It is also a plant and it is completely safe, but if you want to do a magic trick back home, this will amaze everyone . . .' And he proceeded to explain.

Felix listened, wide-eyed with wonder.

'That really is the most fantastic thing I have ever heard!' he said, when Bibi had finished.

'I think even Miss Flora Small will be impressed by that,' Zed said, 'don't you, man?'

CHAPTER 21

A VERY SPECIAL PRESENT

Felix was very sad to say goodbye to Bibi, Mo and Elvis.

They spent a night at Bibi's house again on their way back to the airport and had a lovely evening chatting about their adventures and eating more of the delicious *bogobe* they had had on their first stay.

'I don't want to go home,' Felix sighed. He was sitting on the floor after dinner with Kabelo on his lap. 'I will miss Botswana. And I will miss you too, Kabelo,' he cooed as he stroked the mongoose's soft, stripy fur.

'How can you miss *him*?' Mo scoffed. 'You hardly know him.'

'Yes, but he's so cute and we don't have banded mongoose in England,' said Felix.

Mo stuck her nose in the air and said carelessly, 'Well, if I was a tourist, and if I had made good friends with a Botswanan person, I think I would miss the Botswanan person more than a stupid mongoose. But perhaps you have lots of Botswanan people as your friends back in England?'

Felix looked up and saw that Mo's eyes had gone a bit shiny. 'I – I will miss you too, Mo,' he said quietly. He realized as he said it that he really did mean it. Mo might have got him into trouble, but she had been fun. He would probably never see her again.

Mo glanced at Felix and shot him a mischievous

grin. 'I will miss you too, English Boy Friend!' she said, laughing her raucous hyena-laugh.

Mum had reluctantly agreed to having Flo round the day after they got back from holiday.

Felix was a bundle of nervous excitement.

'What shall I say? Shall I show her the present before she goes mad cos I haven't got a monkey? Shall I show her the film of the monkeys all dressed up to explain how naughty they were?'

Felix remembered what Dad did when he had a speech to practise: he would walk up and down talking to himself, shaking his head, jabbing his finger in the air and muttering until he got the speech exactly right. He called it Blue-Sky Thinking or Brain-Storming, both of which sounded quite uncomfortable and a little bit scary to Felix, but Dad said it worked every time.

So Felix muttered and paced and jabbed his finger in the air. He soon discovered that practising speeches was a lot harder than it looked.

'Hi, Flo. I've got so much to tell you. But first, I want to show you something really cool! . . . Hi, Flo. I've got so many showthings to say you. But first let me cool you how many tellings I've got . . . Hi, Flo. I'm so cool! But first tell me how many somethings you've got—'

DRIIIING!!!

'ARGHH!' Felix leaped in the air. The doorbell was ringing so furiously that even Dyson did not do his usual enthusiastic charge down the hall to see who it was. He hovered, whimpering behind Felix instead.

'I know!' whispered Felix. 'I'm scared too!'

DRIIIIIINNNNNNGGG!

'ARE YOU GOING TO LET ME IN OR NOT?' said a shrill voice.

'Felix!' Mum called from upstairs. 'For goodness sake answer the door, won't you?'

'Yeah, squirt,' said Merv, coming up behind him and thumping him on the shoulder. 'It's probably your *girlfriend*.'

Felix kicked out at his brother, muttering,

199

'Shuddup!' then ran to open the door.

'Oh! HelloFlocomeinandshowmesomethingcool!' he gabbled.

'What are you on about?' barked Flo. 'You'd better have something cool to show *me*.'

Merv snorted and said, 'Going to let your girlfriend boss you around, are you, squirt?' Then he laughed nastily and headed upstairs, from where the sound of thudding music could soon be heard.

Felix rolled his eyes. 'Don't listen to Merv,' he said. Then he stepped back to let Flo past him. 'You'd better come into the kitchen. We have to stay Under The Radar, cos Mum and Dad are tired,' he explained.

'Yes,' said Flo airily. 'It must have been hard work looking after the baby monkey on the aeroplane.' Then she batted her eyelashes at Felix. 'But it will all have been worth it. I do soooo appreciate it,' she added, in her most annoying I-am-such-a- grown-up voice.

Felix swallowed hard. 'Ah, yes,' he said. 'About the baby monkey . . .'

Flo waited, hands on hips, one eyebrow arched.

Felix coughed.

Flo frowned.

Felix shuffled his feet and said, 'The thing is . . .'

Flo glared at him. 'You haven't got one, have you? Honestly, I ask you to do One Simple Thing.' She made as though to leave. 'Well, you know what I said – no monkey, no—'

'No-nonono,' Felix said, jumping between Flo and the door. 'I've got you something much better. I'm going to show you some African magic.'

Flo curled her lip. 'Felix, do you think I am stupid?' she sneered. 'There is No Such Thing as magic. Honestly, even Miss Millie-I'm-A-Duh-Brain Hampton knows *that*.'

'I thought you and Millie were Best Friends now,' said Felix.

Flo flared her nostrils. 'Me? And Millie Hampton? Best Friends?' she scoffed. 'Me and that stupid pink girlie loser who thinks it's OK to have a party and invite Sophie Disbry and *not me*? Best Friends? I think NOT!'

'O-kaaay,' said Felix. 'Anyway, so as I was saying, I have learned some African magic. I can prove it. Then, if you like it, I can show you how it is done. First of all, get me a lemon from that bowl.'

Flo sighed impatiently. She stomped over to the bowl, picked up a lemon and threw it at Felix.

Felix caught it. He was a bit excited now, so he just ignored Flo's bad temper. He turned away briefly then he turned back and said in his Magician Voice.

'I will now perform for you a Once In A Lifetime Amazing African Trick!' Then he did a fake drum roll.

'Oh, for goodness sake, I'm going home,' said Flo.

'No! Watch!' Felix said. Then, with a flourish, he held the lemon in front of his face – and took a massive bite out of it!

Flo's expression turned from shock, to disgust, to

amazement as she watched Felix happily chomp his way through the whole lemon without flinching. In fact, he seemed actually to enjoy eating it.

'WHA –?' she cried. 'Give me that!' she said as she lunged at the small piece of lemon remaining in Felix's hand. She peered at it, sniffed it and then made to take a bite.

'NO!' Felix shouted, flinging his hand out to stop her.

It was too late. Flo had taken a bite.

'Peuh! Bleurgh! YEEEUUUCK!' she cried, throwing the lemon on the floor, spitting and coughing. 'What a horrible trick to play!' she shouted. She ran to the sink and turned the tap on hard. She grabbed a glass, filled it with water and downed it in one go. 'You let me believe the lemon was a sweet or a cake or . . .' she gasped, wiping drips of water from her chin.

'No, I didn't,' said Felix, feeling quite triumphant and calm now. 'That is just what you thought because you watched me eat it.'

'B-but how could you eat such a disgusting thing?' Flo said.

'I told you – African magic,' he said, shrugging.

Flo abruptly stopped her spitting and shouting and stared at Felix. 'Hang on a minute,' she said. 'I don't believe in magic. Show me how you did it.'

'We-ell,' said Felix, hesitating. 'That depends.' He was enjoying the relatively rare experience of being In Control while Flo was around.

'On what?' Flo spat the words out, but Felix saw a glitter of desperation entered her eyes.

'On one condition,' said Felix triumphantly.

'Oh for goodness sake!' cried Flo.

Felix went on. 'It depends on whether you will forget about asking me to steal monkeys *ever again*.'

'Hmm,' said Flo.

 204

'And on whether you want to go on being friends with the Pink Brigade instead of being friends with me,' he added. (It was his turn to be On A Roll now, he thought.)

'Fine, fine. Tell me,' demanded Flo, with a toss of her head.

So Felix dug down into his pockets and brought out a handful of small red berries. 'These,' he said, 'are Miracle Berries. They are special berries I picked in Africa.'

Flo blanched. 'You must *never* eat berries that you have just found In The Wild!' she gasped. 'It's super-dangerous. You might be poisoned!'

Felix grinned. 'It's fine – Mum and Zed know all about this. I didn't just find them by accident, our friend Bibi showed me where to pick them. They're perfectly safe. And they are also magic! If you eat one, everything else that you eat for the rest of the day will taste sweet. Even something normally bitter and disgusting like a lemon or some vinegar.'

'Yeah, right,' said Flo. She forced herself to sound

ever so slightly sarcastic (but Felix thought she actually looked a bit scared). 'And *I* am the Queen.'

Felix shrugged. 'Suit yourself,' he said. 'You saw me eat a lemon, didn't you?'

Flo frowned. 'That could just be that you happen to like eating lemons. You are mad enough.'

Felix sighed. 'Well, I was going to let you try. But if you're too scared, of course . . .'

Flo immediately blushed and said quickly, 'No way! I am not a scaredy-cat, Felix. Give me a berry right this minute.'

Felix held up one of the small red berries. Flo gulped. 'It better *not* be poisonous, Felix,' she said.

'Or my dad will come round here and personally kill you, you know that?'

Felix nodded. 'I promise you that Bibi, Mum and Zed said these berries are safe. Now, when you have eaten the berry, you have to sip this,' he said, handing her a bottle of vinegar.

Flo's eyes opened very, very wide,

but she was determined not to back out now. 'OK,' she said.

She chewed the berry carefully, her little button nose wrinkling. 'Doesn't taste of much – kind of tangy . . .' Then she raised the bottle of vinegar to her lips, took a swift sip, swallowed and closed her eyes.

A small, sly smile spread across her features as the vinegar was transformed into the most delicious drink she had ever had.

'Felix,' she said. 'This is the best present in the world!'

Felix beamed. 'So we are still friends?' he asked.

Flo grinned. 'You betcha!' she said.

'I am sorry about the baby monkey,' Felix added sheepishly.

Flo shook her head. Then she added, with a glint in her eye. 'Who needs a baby monkey when they have a Foolproof Way of getting their own back on Millie-the-Pain Hampton and Sophie-the-Soppy-Idiot Disbry?'

EPILOGUE

Felix snuggled into the corner of the sofa with a contented sigh.

'OK, is everyone ready?' Dad asked.

Zed and Silver had come round, and so had Flo. They were going to watch the films that Felix had made on safari.

Flo had been acting a little bit grumpy as she felt that Felix was Showing Off about his holiday when he had invited her round to see the film, but when Silver arrived with a mound of freshly baked brownies and a huge bowl of strawberries, she soon perked up.

'Mind you, with those Miracle Berries I could have

served you raw onions and limes and you would have tucked in!' Silver joked.

Dad connected the camera to the TV and set the film rolling.

The scenes of the camp and all the animals Felix had seen had come out really well. Flo watched openmouthed when the lionesses with their cubs came on to the screen.

Then suddenly the film became wobblier and less focused.

'This is the monkey part,' Felix hissed. He was slightly disappointed that Mum had made him cut the section where she was getting dressed and Zed was in the shower. Then again, he had not wanted Flo to witness the scene of him on the loo either . . .

Then there they were: the naughty monkeys, dressed head to toe in Mum and Zed's clothes, jabbering at the camera, for all the world laughing and partying as if they were people.

'Wow,' Flo breathed. 'They do look crazy.'

Felix nodded. 'So you see why I couldn't bring you one home?'

Flo pulled a face. 'Not really,' she said. 'It would have been fun.'

'NO, FLO!' everyone chorused.

'There is absolutely no way I am getting into any more monkey madness with you ever again,' said Felix with feeling.

'Okaaay,' said Flo slowly. Then she turned to Felix with an extremely mischievous glint in her eye.

Felix recognized that look. He shuddered as Flo leaned in and whispered, 'I like the look of that banded mongoose in your film. I wonder where we can get one of *those*?'

A MESSAGE FROM THE AUTHOR

As soon as I arrived in Botswana I knew I had to write about the place. The colours, the smells, the sounds of the wildlife, the warmth of the people – it was magical.

My family and I had decided to visit the country to go on a safari. While we were there we all wrote diaries and scribbled in sketch pads so that we would have a record of the wonderful experiences we shared. My diary developed into a list of ideas for the book that you have just read! I had already written *Monkey Business*, which was about how Felix and Flo wanted to have their own zoo and how they got into trouble when they went to visit a safari park in the UK.

While I was in Botswana I could not stop thinking about what Felix would think if he was there with me. I could just see his eyes growing wide at the sight of lion cubs cuddling up to their mum, or at seeing warthogs rooting around in the red earth for things to eat – and, of course, I knew Felix would LOVE the monkeys!

So *Monkey Madness* is based on the amazing holiday

I had in Botswana, and many of the things I have written about really *did* happen to us: we did see lion cubs up very close, monkeys did steal a can of Coke one day (they did not like the taste and threw it back at us!) and we did camp out and visit a village too.

But best of all we met a kind, warm-hearted man called Bibi, who was our guide. He knew everything there was to know about all the animals, birds and plants, and he told us the most jaw-dropping stories about his life in Africa. He told us about how he canoed to school and had to make a heartbreaking decision about his puppy in order to save his own life.

He also told us about the baobab tree and about how one day his mum found a snake in her car while she was driving. And so this book is dedicated to the real Bibi, who gave us the holiday of a lifetime and taught us things we will never forget. (Just in case you are wondering, he does have a daughter, but she is much younger than Mo – and much, MUCH better behaved!)

Thank you for reading
Love, Anna xxx

GLOSSARY

Dumela, Rra   Good morning, sir

Dumela, Mma   Good morning, madam

Ke a leboga   Thank you

Tambotie   African children play with these special seeds and call them 'jumping beans' because of the moth larvae which live inside the seeds and jump around.

Miracle berries   These berries really do change your sense of taste and the effect lasts for a whole day.

Baobab tree   There are many, many myths and stories about the baobab tree and its place in African culture. In times of severe drought some villages get their water supply from the hundreds of litres of water that can be found in the tap roots of the tree.

I'M A CHICKEN, GET ME OUT OF HERE!

Anna Wilson

Titch the chicken is trapped. She arrived at Wilf's house
by mistake when one of Mum's Internet orders went
wrong (again). Now she is desperate to GET OUT OF THERE!
There's a dopey dog to deal with and a very snooty cat –
and, worse, Wilf has made her share a room with
Brian, an EXTREMELY fussy guinea pig.

Titch is no birdbrain and plots to escape. But when
the other pets are put in danger, Titch realizes she
has to stay and help her new friends . . .

Welcome to the Pooch Parlour, where mystery-solving has become this season's hottest new look!

Anna Wilson

Something very strange is going on in the cosy town of Crumbly-under-Edge! Join Pooch Parlour regulars Dash the dachshund and his human friend Pippa 'chat-till-the-cows-come-home' Peppercorn as they uncover a dastardly plot involving oodles of snooty poodles . . .

Collect all three in the bonkers Pooch Parlour series!

DO YOU LOVE ANIMALS TOO?

If so I'd love to hear from you. Write to me at:

ANNA WILSON
C/O MACMILLAN CHILDREN'S BOOKS
20 NEW WHARF ROAD
LONDON N1 9RR
UNITED KINGDOM

Remember to enclose your full name and
postal address (not your email address) so
that I know where to write back to!
And please do not send me any
photos or drawings
unless you are
happy for me
to keep them.

Anna xxx